THE SHAPES OF WRATH

HOPE'S SEVEN DEADLY SINS THRILLER 1:
WRATH

MELISSA YI

For Ming-Ka,
With special thanks
for your precise attention
to detail.
Cheers,
M

Windtree
Press

For the resident who got punched

Join Melissa's mailing list at www.myi.ninja

Published by Olo Books in association with Windtree Press
Printed in Canada on 100% recycled paper

Yi, Melissa, author The Shapes of Wrath / Melissa Yi. (Hope's Seven Deadly Sins Thriller; 1)
Issued in print and electronic formats.
ISBN (softcover) 978-1-998758-01-2.--ISBN (eBook) 978-1-998758-02-9
I. Title. C813'.6

To advise of typographical errors, please contact olobooks@gmail.com

Anesthesia is the half-awake watching the half-asleep being half-murdered by the half-witted.

— Anonymous

Do I shock you? We are very playful here. It's a good tone for an operating theater. It is a theater, after all.

— David Cronenberg

Anger is an expensive luxury in which only men of certain income can indulge.

— George William Curtis

PROLOGUE

UNIVERSITY COLLEGE HOSPITAL, MONTREAL, CANADA

GORDON

September 14, 07:58

Gordon Cole didn't expect anyone to die that day.

He'd chosen anesthesia as a specialty one year ago partly because 99 percent of the time, everything flowed smoothly in the operating room.

As a junior resident doctor, Gordon helped put patients to sleep for surgery, kept them alive during the procedure, and gently brought them back to consciousness afterward. His epidurals eased the pain of childbirth so much that one new mother named her baby after him. Gordon helped wean chronic pain patients off dangerously high doses of narcotics. Ninety-nine percent of the time, anesthesia stayed calm and well-controlled.

The other one percent of the time, the patient crashed before his eyes. A woman's airway swelled shut, blocking her breathing. A man bled out after a stab wound to his heart. Worst of all, a baby with an abnormal connection between her trachea and esophagus had choked in front of him.

Then anesthesia had to control the airway and breathing, support the circulation, and take control of the situation.

That terrified Gordon. Luckily, today's attending physician, Dr. Burns, handled pretty much everything.

Everything except the world's meanest surgeon.

Gordon got along with most surgeons. Some of them joked non-stop. Nearly all saved lives on the regular. Gordon especially admired the skill of two female attending surgeons.

But the one dinosaur left in Canada dwelled at Montreal's University College Hospital.

"Come on, Singlit!" shouted Dr. Vrac before kicking the OR table hard enough to jostle the unconscious patient, Joan Finn.

Mrs. Finn's sedated body didn't stir more than a centimetre, but the scrub nurse, Trent, gasped.

"I'm right here," replied Raj Singh, the general surgery chief resident at Dr. Vrac's side.

"I'm getting old waiting for the all-clear," said Dr. Vrac. He watched the anesthesiologist, eyes glittering, without picking on Dr. Burns directly.

Dr. Burns kept his lips pressed together as he double-checked the patient's endotracheal tube, the tube that allowed Mrs. Finn to breathe during the surgery, and the CO_2 *monitor that measured her carbon dioxide level.*

"Stinks in here, gas docs," Dr. Vrac told the anaesthesia team, sniffing the air through his mask while the surgical staff gathered around Mrs. Finn's lower half on the operating room table. "I haven't even used the cautery yet. Anyone else smell that?"

The stench filled the confines of their white-walled room. It didn't smell like inhalational agents like Sevoflurane, nor like cauterized, or burnt, tissue. Gordon shifted side to side and held his breath as he stood with Dr. Burns at the patient's head and neck on one side of the blue drape. The surgical staff on the opposite side of the drape didn't flinch at the smell of ... well, human gas.

Dr. Burns privately called the blue drape the "blood-brain barrier," a joke both about the membrane separating the brain from the rest of the body and the fact that surgeons might deal with the flesh and blood, but anesthesiologists considered themselves the true brains of the OR.

"Someone's *got a bad case of the farts today," said Dr. Vrac. "As a general surgeon, I'm an expert in that. Pus, guts, or cancer, I'm your man!" He turned to his chief resident. "Too much daal, eh, Dr. Singh?"*

Gordon winced. The curly-haired medical student tsked, but the scrub nurse, Trent, snorted and laughed. Singh shook his head and kept his gloved hands sterile by pressing his palms together as if in prayer.

"Running behind today?" Tammy called from the doorway. As the charge nurse, she made sure every OR ran on time.

"No way," Vrac shot back. "Just about to blow the belly up." He cackled as if no one had ever heard his slang for inflating the abdomen with carbon dioxide for laparoscopic surgery.

"Almost there," said Dr. Burns, double checking a wire.

Gordon knew better than to elbow his way in as a first year anesthesia resident. He'd run cases alone, but never with Dr. Vrac. Dr. Burns—who didn't invite Gordon to call him by his first name, Bob—would tell Gordon if he wanted his help. Right now, Gordon stayed out of the way.

"Might be done faster if we had an RT today, Tammy," said Dr. Vrac.

Gordon scowled behind his blue surgical mask. At UC Hospital, the respiratory therapist often assisted on the airway, but the ORs ran one RT short today. Dr. Burns had told Tammy that he and Gordon could manage on their own.

"Want me to donate another 20K to the foundation to speed this up? Consider it done. I can always make more money." Dr. Vrac wiggled his gloved fingers in the air. "Surgical hands. Magic *hands. Girls love 'em. That's why I've got more women than cars."*

"So magical that he has no wife," Dr. Burns whispered. He and Gordon exchanged a silent moment of understanding on their side of the drape before the older anesthesiologist let out an unmistakable ripping noise.

"Fart attack!" Dr. Vrac laughed so hard that he almost fell onto the unconscious patient.

"Excuse me," Dr. Burns muttered, but no one else heard him while Dr. Vrac shouted, "Instead of Robbie Burns day, it's Farty Burns day!"

The humiliation writ large on Dr. Burns's face was Gordon's first clue that someone might die today.

1

MAY 22, 08:40 (NINE MONTHS LATER)

ST. JOSEPH'S HOSPITAL, MONTREAL, CANADA

HOPE

"You got the death OR, Hope," said the medical student, a short guy I vaguely recognized.

"The death OR." I strode down the dim hallway toward the operating rooms. "You mean OR 3?"

"Yep." He pushed away the brown curls flopping into his eyes. "Gotta go. I'm with Dr. Pierce, and she's fierce." He shoved open the door to OR 1 while a nurse detoured around him with a tray.

Dang. The early bird gets the worm, and the late resident wins the Operating Room of Doom?

I avoid bad juju. Partly it's an Asian thing untempered by the fact that I was born in Canada. But doctors in general lean on science with a teaspoon of superstition, and nurses will outright blame the full moon for a nutty night shift.

Maybe that med student was playing me. Although I outranked him as an M.D. and family medicine resident on what used to be called an internship year, some young'uns don't show proper manners.

My shoes echoed down the grey hallway as I unpocketed my cell phone to call Dr. John Tucker, the one guy I know who hoovers up the gossip. "Hey, babe."

"Hi, Hope." Tucker sounded wary, as befitted an ex-fiancé. I should've left him alone, but a) I still love him (aaargh), and b) we work together as residents at Montreal's St. Joseph's Hospital, although currently on parallel rotations, me gen surg (general surgery), him Ob/gyn (obstetrics and gynecology).

"I just heard that OR 3 is, ah, unlucky," I told Tucker.

His sigh flooded my speaker. "You got 'Flee OR 3'?"

"Apparently."

"You never heard of Dr. Vrac, the VIP of OR 3?"

"Let me guess. He has bad *qi.*" I could rhyme too while I paused outside OR 3. Through the small window in the beige door, I spotted a white man bellowing at everyone trapped inside with him. Not young, from the bags under his eyes and the grey hair under his surgical cap, but a reasonably fit build under his worn-in scrubs. Dr. Vrac, I presume.

Tucker chuckled, which made my toes tingle despite the horror lurking before me, and my former guy invented another quasi poem. "I'll spill the tea. He'll make you pee."

Tea meant gossip, and pee made me think of our bestie, Tori Yamamoto, currently on an elective in urology. Tori also has a special gift beyond medicine: she speaks to ghosts. Hard to believe, but the mere thought of it pricked the hair on my arms. "The truth shall imprison me."

"'Bye-bye and good luck, *ma cherie.*"

I laughed and muffed up my last rhyme. *"Oui oui oui.* Do re mi." I hung up and shoved open that door.

Dr. Vrac swore loud enough to blow the hair back from my head if I hadn't been wearing one of those attractive blue bonnets myself. His head canted to one side, zombie-style. "Who the hell are you? You from Roy's Car Service?"

I forced a smile behind my surgical mask. "Dr. Hope Sze, family med R1." That meant family medicine first year resident. "First day on general surgery."

A portly nurse with bleached hair nodded at me before she left the room without introducing herself. I belatedly nodded back.

Dr. Vrac cackled. "Tammy doesn't like you."

"I'm sorry to hear that," I said evenly. A good doctor won't get fazed by swearing surgeons and neutral nurses. "How can I help?"

"Can you do a laparoscopic hernia repair better than the piece of shit residents I got working for me?" Vrac barked a laugh and waited for everyone else to join in.

The scrub nurse tittered on command. I'm 27, but she looked younger, maybe 22.

"You like that, Delilah?" Vrac leered behind his mask. "Wanna ride my Mercedes?"

Delilah raised her blond eyebrows at the other nurses for help before she shrugged in confusion.

"I always keep an extra car around for the ladies. Here, watch this. Singh!"

The tall, very thin resident glanced up with gorgeous, dark eyes. My friend Ginger loves guys with an "arachnoid" build. I'd have to introduce her to Dr. Raj Singh, whom I recognized as the chief resident.

"Singh, take over the case so I can go for a ride with Delilah and—what's your name, honey? Sneeze?"

I opened my mouth and closed it before I shook my head. "No, Hope Sze. Like the letter C." I prefer the *Tse* sound, but this man required easy mode.

He ignored it. "Sounds like a good band name, right? Vrac and the Delilah Sneeze!"

Delilah laughed weakly. I frowned, which made no difference to Vrac.

"I'll take you out right now. Where are we?"

"Final inspection and closure," said the shorter, stockier, Asian resident. His eyes crinkled at me above his mask, and I liked him right away. He must be Dr. Mark Cheng, the urology resident doing time on general surgery.

Vrac sighed. "Aww, you came right at the end, Sneeze. You want to scrub in and help suture?"

My heart thumped. "Yes, please."

"Perfect. See you soon."

I hurried out the door and washed my hands before using the waterless scrub. Despite our sinks with running water, most places, even St. Joe's, have switched over to an alcohol-based scrub, like hand sanitizer, that requires intricate cleaning from the fingernails to the arms.

"You're doing it wrong," said a woman's voice behind me.

"Oh. Sorry. This is how they taught me in London." I spun around to face Tammy, the neutral blond charge nurse "who doesn't like you," with my hands in the air.

"Start again and show me," she said.

I reached for the dispensing pump.

"No. Wash and dry your hands and clean your nails."

Ooh boy. I restarted at the beginning.

"There are eight steps to the waterless scrub. Can you name them for me?"

Getting pimped by the charge nurse. "One. Wash and dry your hands and clean your nails. Two. Pump one squirt into the palm. Three—"

"Stay with one."

I demonstrated my nail and hand cleaning to her in excruciating detail before pressing on the pump.

"Only one time. Otherwise, you'll have to restart."

I scrubbed my nails and cuticles, trying not to peer in the little window. They'd finish the case any second now.

The door flapped open. Vrac stared at me before he laughed and threw an arm around each of us, looping us together with me on his left side. He smelled like cologne and used deodorant. "Tammy and Sneeze! What are you doing here?"

I kept my hands in the air. "Scrubbing in."

"I'm teaching your little resident how to scrub in properly," Tammy said.

"Good job, but we're done now. Singh's dictating. Better luck next time. You listen to everything Tammy says, all right? She's the boss."

I nodded, holding my breath so I wouldn't have to smell him. Tammy issued a tight-lipped nod.

Vrac murmured, "Good." His left hand cupped my bum cheek, giving it a quick squeeze.

I whirled toward him, mouth open, but he'd already slipped away so fast that his bonnet ties flapped in the breeze as he called, "Great working with you!"

2

MAY 22, 08:56

HOPE

"You okay?" someone asked.

I blinked, tracking the source of that voice. A brown-skinned man, his greying hair peeking out from his scrub cap, wheeled the patient out of the OR.

"I didn't die," I managed to say. That must be a win for OR 3.

Vrac grabbed my ass.

No one else saw him.

He'll deny it.

"I'm Dr. Burns, the anesthesiologist," the man said, rolling the patient toward the recovery room. "Come see me if you need to."

"Thanks." I tried to shake off my worry. I had to work with Dr. Vrac for the next four weeks.

No other doctor had ever laid hands on me before. None of my friends had mentioned it either. Nobody did this in the 21st century.

Okay, maybe the occasional patient with dementia. But no other supervising physicians I knew.

A ring tone like a race car engine roared from the end of the hall. Vrac barked into his phone, "Roy! Do my X5."

"It's okay. Breathe," said Mark Cheng, the junior surgical resident who now stood on my right.

"And make sure it's mineral white, not alpine. Why not, you SOB?" Vrac shouted into his cell phone.

OR 3, SOB. And I don't mean short of breath.

I raised my eyebrows at Mark.

"We all go through it," he said.

Really? Did he grope guys too? I opened my mouth to ask.

"It's a hazing. He's not all bad. Someone from your hospital foundation came into the lounge to personally thank him for his $50,000 donation last week."

Uh oh. I made a face. St. Joe's would never get rid of a moneybag like Vrac, no matter how many residents he abused.

"We figure he must've been dumped by a thousand women. Don't worry, he'll forget about you," said Mark, glancing through the door at Delilah.

Hurt people hurt. Premed Hope vowed compassion and tried to save worms marooned on the pavement on a rainy day. Present day Hope wanted to hurt Vrac back. If Vrac moved onto Delilah, I'd try to protect her too.

"He usually picks on the doctors," said Mark, reading my mind. "Nurses and other staff have unions. Doctors and medical students ... "

He left it unsaid, but I knew enough to fill in the blanks. MDs and MDs in training have the university, which cares about its own income and reputation, and will cheerfully flay us if it will get them ten cents on the dollar or another thumbs up on social media.

"Anyway, I'm Mark Cheng, off-service urology R2." Mark clasped my hand hard. "Call me Cheng. Makes it easier because that's what Vrac does."

"Thanks. Hope Sze. Not sneeze," I added under my breath.

"Gotcha." Cheng waved through the window at the chief resident who dictated the operative note in the OR's side room. "That's Singh, the gen surg chief resident. Let me show you the OR lounge. That's where the surgeons hang out between cases, with the coffee."

"Cool." I could use more orientation. I'd already figured out how to swipe into the locked operating area with my badge, step on the mat to activate the door, cover my hair and shoes, grab a pair of scrubs from the change room, and shove an extra set of gloves in my back pocket. Too bad those gloves hadn't dissuaded Dr. Vrac. "Is that the lounge?" I asked, pointing at a door back toward the entrance.

He snorted. "That's the junk room where they shove all the crap no one wants. Whatever doesn't fit in the central storage room at the back, where all the ORs are connected." He gave me a strange look. "You didn't know that?"

"How would I know that?"

"Right, family medicine," he said, which stung.

"I wanted to do plastics," I told him before I bit my lip.

He looked sympathetic. "Didn't match?"

"Nope." I was the only student who declined THC gummies at a surgery party and got branded "not a team player." Coincidence or not, in the grand scramble at the end of med school, I ended up matching to family medicine instead of plastics.

"Well, you can do Botox and filler as a family doctor."

I grimaced. "No, I like hands and microsurgery. The month before I came on, a pregnant woman fell from a height and cut her arm off. Successful replant." Translation: they sewed her arm back on!

Cheng gave a low whistle. "Cool case. We'll never see that at St. Joe's—traumas go straight to UC Hospital—but we've got six ORs. Pretty busy for a community hospital." He pointed at the last three doors at the end of the hall. "Nurses' lounge is the biggest one on the left, attached to the women's change room. We're on the right, attached to the men's change room, before the anesthesia lounge. Anesthesia's fridge broke last week—"

I rolled my eyes. More proof that everything sucks at St. Joe's.

"—so they're in and out of our fridge all the time. It's no big deal, surgery and anesthesia shared a lounge at UC. But make sure you label your lunch."

"Done."

Cheng held the door open for me. I stepped into a room like our residents' lounge, only bigger, with windows, two landline phones instead of one, and best of all, didn't smell like old spaghetti and shoes. Both men and women, in a 65/35 split, sat on the couch near the TV or stood to check their phones. One older surgeon read the newspaper. Another poured himself a cup of coffee.

"Hang on. I'll grab my water." Cheng threw open the fridge door, pushing aside a yellow lunch bag labelled R. BURNS, clearly owned by the anesthetist who had spoken to me after Vrac's ass attack.

Cheng greeted his friends, downed some water, and checked his watch. "Let's beat Vrac back."

I exhaled. Vrac was my overlord for the next four weeks. I must see and obey.

"I can show you the way to stores," said Cheng, teasing me about how I didn't know the storage area in the OR, so I nudged him. Surgeons are big jokers, except Vrac.

Back in OR 3, Cheng pointed at the cutout in the wall at the back. "That's where we keep the good stuff. Surgical equipment, mesh, catheters, splints ... you name it, we got it. And don't worry about the ghost rumors. Haven't seen any yet." Cheng checked his watch again and frowned at the empty operating table.

"The *ghost* rumors?" I repeated. I did get a weird vibe in this room. "What do you mean?"

The OR door slammed open.

Vrac glowered at both of us from the doorway, fists clenched. "Where is anesthesia."

My mouth fell open. He must mean Dr. Burns, but Cheng and I hadn't hidden him anywhere.

"Has anyone seen Dr. Burns?" An Asian man in glasses and navy scrubs entered the OR. His badge said Andy, and I noticed a few syringes in his front pocket, so he was either a doctor, a nurse, or a respiratory therapist (RT).

Silence. I glanced at Singh, now hovering silently in the doorway behind Vrac. Singh shook his head, making me stay mute.

Vrac advanced on me and Cheng. "You deaf?"

"I think Dr. Burns went to the break room," said Mimi, a white nurse wearing a wild surgical cap with dolls printed on it.

"Yeah? And did he forget how to tell time while he was at it?"

Silence. I tried to maintain a placid expression.

Dr. Vrac snarled, actually snarled, at me and Cheng.

"I'll find him," said Cheng smoothly. "It would be my pleasure."

"On it," said Singh, already spinning around to go.

Vrac marched to the doorway and hollered at their backs, "Bring him back here so he can start the case five minutes ago!"

I slipped the opposite way, toward the storage room. I wouldn't find Dr. Burns unless he'd needed to replace a monitor, but hiding from Vrac took higher priority.

Stores turned out to be a cavernous room filled with, well, everything. Wire storage bins lined the walls, the bins stacked in rows like a library of equipment. Monitors clustered together in the middle of the room.

I glanced over my shoulder to make sure Vrac hadn't followed me. 'Cause the only thing worse than Vrac was alone time with Vrac.

The storage area felt empty. Even ... haunted.

"Dr. Burns?" I called. My voice didn't echo off the white walls. Too much stuff shoved in here, absorbing sound waves. "Dr. Burns?"

I kept moving. If Vrac snuck up behind me, I should look busy and stay out of ass-grabbing range.

I could have exited through one of the other ORs that branched out in all directions, arteries leading away from this central heart of a storage area, except the last thing they needed during an active OR was a stray resident dashing through their operations, shouting for Dr. Burns.

Then I'd end up as the laughing stock, as well as the handmaiden for Dr. Vrac.

One closet door stood slightly ajar. Light shone around the edge of the door frame.

Who'd left the light on? I reached for the door handle, and as soon as I pulled, a man's scrub-clad body rolled toward me.

3

SEPTEMBER 14, 08:08

GORDON

"I've got to go," Dr. Burns told Gordon in a low, urgent voice. The man had never audibly passed gas before. He looked sweaty, unlike his usual impassive self.

"Belly up." Dr. Vrac gestured to inflate the patient's abdomen before he instructed the most junior member of his team, "Watch and learn, medical student. You need something in that curly head besides cholesterol guidelines."

"I'll handle it," Gordon whispered to his supervisor, who moved toward the door.

Dr. Vrac cackled from his position at the patient's midsection while he accepted an instrument, his eyes glued to the screen. "What's wrong with you, Burnsie? You'll never get a Tesla like that. You can't handle a half hour surgery?"

"An hour with you," said Dr. Burns, and Gordon silently rejoiced. Dr. Vrac took twice as long for a laparoscopic cholecystectomy as most surgeons, probably because he insulted Singh every other minute.

Dr. Burns nodded at Gordon. "I'll be back soon."

Gordon eyed the monitors, noting all the parameters within normal limits.

"We're in trouble now!" said Vrac as he manipulated the instrument in the patient's abdomen. "Good thing I'm on the case."

Gordon kept his mouth shut. He stuttered under stress.

"Dream come true, right, baby anesthesia? Let the surgeon do the work while you sit there with your Sudoku, right, son?"

Gordon flushed. Surgeons couldn't work without anesthesia unless Dr. Vrac time travelled to a battlefield where screaming patients only got a bullet to bite on.

While Gordon contemplated some good comebacks, a monitor beeped. Gordon frowned at the numbers flashing on the screen: 30. 29. 27. 28.

"Shut up," said Vrac automatically, like he was swatting a fly.

"It's the CO2 monitor." Gordon silenced it. He pressed his lips together and tried to concentrate as it kept flashing: 27. 25. 24.

Why would the patient's carbon dioxide level drop? Was he hyperventilating the patient, forcing her to exhale too much CO2? Or had her cardiac output dropped, her heart pumping less blood into her circulation?

Gordon cycled the blood pressure cuff so he could keep a closer eye on her BP while scanning her other vital signs and eyeballing her electrocardiogram.

Then he tapped the screen to check her carbon dioxide levels from the beginning of the case. The computer stored every patient's data. Today, maybe it was Dr. Vrac's glare, maybe it was the residual stink in the OR, but his sweaty fingers fumbled before he found her original numbers, 38 to 42. Big change.

"Something's wrong," Gordon mumbled. He checked the circuit for a leak, even though a disconnect should lose the tracing altogether.

"I'll tell you what's wrong." Vrac didn't take his eyes off the video monitor as he continued to operate. "Your dick's too small."

Everyone else laughed while Gordon thumbed the silence button again.

He double-checked and triple-checked the circuit. No leak. No problem with the endotracheal tube.

Gordon cleared his throat. "No, something else is wrong. The CO2. I think ... you need to deflate the abdomen."

"What?"

"Deflate the abdomen," Gordon repeated as loudly as he dared. The

inflated abdomen allowed the surgeons to see the organs during the operation, but in rare cases, the CO_2 *could escape into the patient's bloodstream.*

That got Vrac's attention. He glared at Gordon, who felt himself shrinking even before the surgeon spit out, "I've barely started! What's wrong with you!"

It's the best thing for the patient, *Gordon struggled to say. He'd been taught that if the surgeons argued with you, you circled back to putting the patient first. Surgeons couldn't argue with that.*

"The p-p-patient is—" Gordon started, but another monitor began to beep, higher pitched now. Gordon hunted for the new cause and found it right away. "—t-t-tachycardic now, 112."

"So? I could do that in my sleep. I bet I hit 112 when I back my BMW out of my driveway. I started Crossfit. Me. At 62—"

"Heart rate 125," Gordon mumbled. The heart beats faster under stress. If the patient's blood pressure crashed too, it meant shock or cardiovascular collapse, not Crossfit.

Why couldn't Gordon speak up? Although he'd covered patients alone from day 1 of his anesthesia residency, and even during medical school, no one rattled him as badly as Dr. Vrac. The other surgeons listened *when the patients crashed.*

"Heart rate 128," Gordon said. "And it looks irregular."

"How can you tell with a heart rate of 128?" Vrac said before he added, "Singh, go look at the monitors."

"I'm scrubbed in," Singh said.

"I didn't tell you to scrub out. Just take a peek and we can keep doing the case."

Gordon could use another doctor's opinion. He swung his monitor almost 180 degrees to let Dr. Singh read it from the surgical side of the drape.

"Blood pressure low," said Singh, his hands clasped to avoid contamination. "Wasn't she hypertensive at the beginning of the case?"

"Yes, 159 on 98," said Gordon.

"Well, now she's 86 on 40, heart rate's popping up to 133. And her CO_2*—"*

Gordon cranked the oxygen to 100 percent and pushed Phenylephrine to raise the blood pressure as sweat trickled down his back. "I'm s-s-sure it's a CO2 embolus. Deflate!"

"No way!" shouted Vrac, but Singh's arm moved, probably for the gas inflow valve, while the circulating nurse rushed into the hallway to find Dr. Burns.

"What did I just say!" Vrac bawled.

Gordon issued orders to save Joan Finn's life. "T-t-turn her on her left side in T-Trendelenberg. I'll s-s-start an IJ to s-suction the embolus. You p-page Dr. B-Burns s-s-stat to OR 3."

4

MAY 22, 09:09

HOPE

For a split second, I stared at the man crumpled at my feet. Two things struck me: the unnatural grey cast to his brown skin and the crooked badge identifying Dr. Robert Burns.

"HELP HELP HELP HELP!" I shouted, dragging Dr. Burns so he stretched full-length onto the floor, on his back.

He didn't breathe. Didn't blink. No heartbeat.

CPR first. No one else around, so I dropped to my knees on his right side, locked my arms, and started chest compressions.

"HELP HELP HELP HELP!" I yelled again, indenting his sternum with each blow.

"What are you—" a woman's voice called back.

"It's Dr. Burns!" I shouted, each word punctuated by a compression. I gasped for breath. "HELP. HELP. HELP. HELP!"

Andy, the RT/nurse/doctor I'd seen earlier, dropped to his knees at Burns's head. "Call a code and get the crash cart! I need an Ambu bag!"

Mimi checked Dr. Burns's arm. "Good vein. Give me an 18, or even a 16!"

"Someone take over CPR!" I panted.

Andy steadied a laryngoscope for the airway. A big guy in a hairnet resumed CPR from the other side of the body as soon as the tube slid in.

"I need Narcan, an amp of Epi, a defibrillator, and a monitor!" I called.

Tammy pulled intranasal Narcan from her breast pocket and swiftly injected it up Dr. Burns's nose before anyone could finish drawing it up from a vial.

Unusual to carry Narcan, but we all should during the opioid crisis. We waited for a tense second before we shook our heads. No response. Compressions hadn't stopped.

"Let's get him up here." A woman rolled up with a gurney.

I frowned. Epi or cardiac monitor should come first, but if we got him on that gurney, we could transport him to a room with all the fixings instead of dragging each item over piecemeal from the crash cart.

"Let's carry him," Andy called, bagging Dr. Burns as he spoke. "He's not moving at all."

To haul him up to waist height, we each reached for a limb. Andy took the head. My back twinged, but I ignored the pain while I climbed onto the stretcher to continue CPR as we flew back to OR 3 where Tammy already held open the door for us.

While I sweated over compressions on the moving stretcher, Andy steered with one hand. He and Mimi, two white guys, and a short Black woman all ran alongside using one hand to hold onto the loaded syringes in their front pockets. I didn't carry meds like that, but assumed it must be an OR thing.

"Come on!" yelled Tammy, who hadn't bothered to help lift him onto the stretcher.

Vrac swept ahead of her, half-blocking the door. "I bet it's drugs. Can't take the heat."

I scowled and jumped down. Hairnet guy took over compressions, Singh grabbed the airway, and Cheng reached for a line while Tammy asked, "Where'd you find him?"

"In stores," I said. "Not breathing, no heart beat. I need an amp of Epi. Continue CPR. Get him on a monitor, O2, two IV's. See if he's in VFib and call a Code Blue."

When Tammy attached the leads, in the seconds before restarting CPR, the monitor still showed a flatline. Asystole.

5

SEPTEMBER 14, 09:33

GORDON

The team at UC Hospital ran the code on Joan Finn long and hard. Dr. Burns returned to OR 3 to issue terse commands. Dr. Vrac argued with him before stalking out of the room.

They stabilized Mrs. Finn enough to get her into the ICU and to call for hyperbaric oxygen, but she died on transfer.

Gordon called the Canadian Medical Protective Association (CMPA), the organization he paid in case he ever got into legal hot water, and the advisor told him to make careful notes about what had happened. Because of the bad outcome (which meant that a patient had died), she'd pass his file onto a lawyer.

"Should I reach out to the family?" Gordon asked. "To tell them I'm sorry?"

"Don't say anything that admits liability. You can offer condolences for their loss if they reach out to you," said the advisor.

"Should I call them?"

"You may want to speak to your lawyer before you make any calls. Write down what happened."

Gordon wrote notes, but what was he supposed to do? Wait until Joan Finn's lawyer served him?

"The less said about it, the better," said Dr. Burns the next day, when they met in the doctors' lounge.

"You don't think if we did M&M rounds—"

"If they do M&M rounds," said Dr. Burns, folding a newspaper and placing it carefully on the table near the TV, "we listen and learn."

Morbidity and Mortality Rounds highlighted cases where patients had suffered significant disease or had died, and the group brainstormed ways the case could have been handled better, not to shame or blame, but to learn. That was the idea, anyway.

"Are you ... feeling better?" Gordon asked hesitantly.

Annoyance crossed Dr. Burns's face. "Never better. I have to go now."

Instead of stopping at the coffee canister the way he normally would, Dr. Burns pushed open the lounge door. When Gordon followed, Dr. Burns ignored him, turning downstairs and heading for the cafeteria.

6

MAY 22, 10:15

HOPE

"Burnsie should've shot up at home," said Dr. Vrac.

I don't cry after a code. My emotions flatten while my brain stays locked at the bedside. So even though I followed the rest of my team out of OR 3, I'd ignored their conversation until now.

Dr. Vrac and the other residents swept into the lounge without me. "Burnsie messed up my case list. Now I'm FUBARred. I was already 13 minutes late starting today."

Yeah, that's a good reaction when your colleague barely dodges death. I rushed after the group, catching the door one second before it locked.

Vrac downed a cup of coffee. Cheng glanced at me and pointed at a cup. Sweet of him, but I gestured for him to take it. He shrugged and finished the pot himself.

Dr. Vrac's head snapped toward a woman heading out the door. "Hey. Hey, Lydia. Can you do my case instead of this one? I need anesthesia." He thrust his coffee at me and sprinted after Lydia, who continued out the door, already shaking her head.

I'd trade cleaning up after him for a few seconds of peace. I exhaled in relief and set his coffee beside the sink.

The chief resident sipped his java and held out his other hand. "Hi, I'm Raj Singh. You can call me Singh." His clasp was gentle, and he let go right away.

What a nice guy. "Sze. Hope Sze if you're being fancy."

Cheng winked at me. "Sometimes we get a little fancy around here."

"We're missing another resident," said Singh. "Veronica Sadler."

"What happened to her?" *Ghost rumors* shot through my mind, but I couldn't repeat that in front of Singh.

Cheng laughed. "Nothing bad. She's on mat leave."

I'd take a baby over Dr. Vrac or ghosts any day. Phew. I grinned back at him.

Singh stayed expressionless, but at least he didn't growl over Dr. Sadler's maternity leave. The other residents do more call when you're a team member short, but residency gives you paid mat leave. Once you graduate, you get shafted. No pension, no parental leave, nothing for MDs. If you're lucky, your provincial association pays you a small stipend for 17 weeks, but it depends on the province and if you've paid enough into the system beforehand. Nothing compared to the 18 *months* parental leave nurses and other employees can receive.

Cheng tapped me on the shoulder. "I get why you'd ask. That was the craziest morning ever."

"Maybe not ever," said Singh, staring off into space.

Before I could ask, Cheng thumped his chest. "Ranks right up there for me. I'm your waterworks guy. Kidneys, ureters, bladders, urethras, and prostates. Anything outside that, including an anesthetist on the floor with no heartbeat? Outside my comfort zone."

I sighed. "Me too." Anyone who says a code is easy, especially a code on your superior, is smoking something. "Except I need to learn more about waterworks too." Medicine is a never-ending story of learning. Sometimes that's cool, but mostly you drink from the fire hose of information twelve hours a day and still feel guilty when you finally hit the sack.

Singh smiled at me. "We'll get some general surgery into you while you're here."

"Fantastic. I love surgery."

"You're a smart woman." He checked his phone. "Smart enough to handle this consult. Go to the ER. A rule out appy patient just got a CT."

"No problem." I like checking if an appendix is hot, not, or in the grey zone. I didn't match to plastics, but I reconciled myself to a better lifestyle in the ER, my new happy place. "Have a good rest."

Singh laughed. "There is no rest."

"He's heading to Galloway's clinic," said Cheng. "He has to finalize the call schedule. We've got 30 inpatients to check labs on—"

"Don't forget studying. And my research."

"And your fellowship application, right?" Cheng nudged Singh's shoulder.

"Oh." I felt like a tool. "Well, good luck with that." I hustled down to ground level. The emerg, as I affectionately call it, lives on the *rez-de-chaussée*, or ground floor in French. Patients in stretchers lay in the hallway, lined up to the vending machine, but not beyond, so an average day for over-capacity. I glanced at the white board: 149% capacity. Not bad!

My favourite nurse, Roxanne, greeted me as soon as I walked in through the automatic doors. "Hope! My hero."

I nudged her good arm. "Back at you. You feeling okay?"

"Awesome." She winked at me. She'd pinned up the other sleeve, not bothering to hide the fact that she was missing part of that arm. "You know that I can hit an IV as fast as my friends with two hands?"

"I have no doubt." I blew her a kiss.

"But enough about me. What hell were you raising this morning?"

I grimaced as I walked to the central nursing station and pulled up the chart of the rule out appy (appendicitis) patient. "Not exactly hell. Dr. Burns made it."

"I know he did, he's in ICU right now, but what happened to him?"

"I don't know. I found him on the floor. ICU should have his tox screen, since there's a question if he overdosed." Toxicology should tell us.

She frowned. "You think that Dr. Burns overdosed?"

"I don't know him at all, but that would be more common than a heart attack or another cause in a relatively young, healthy person. Do you know how old he is?"

She shrugged. "He looked late 50's."

"That's what I thought, too." Although it's harder to tell with a surgical mask and no circulation. If the camera adds ten pounds, no oxygen adds 60 years.

Roxanne tilted her head. "I'd be surprised if he was a user. Not that I can't be fooled, but I have a good gut about that sort of thing."

"I hear you." A useful skill in an ER nurse. Like what used to be called gaydar, only medical, and I'd trust Roxanne for a century before Vrac.

But an overdose would explain why I'd found Dr. Burns on the floor. If you purloin medications, you can easily inject the wrong dose, the wrong drug, or have an allergic reaction and stop breathing.

"We lock up our narcotics," Roxanne pointed out. "Anesthesia would have more access than most, but it's all locked and counted every night."

"I heard that some people withdraw the med and inject sterile water so the vial looks full."

She screwed up her nose. "That's possible, but we'd notice the medication caps missing, and his patients would cry in pain right in front of him."

"Not if he knocked them out, I guess."

We exchanged looks. It's considered torture to paralyze someone without properly sedating them and controlling their pain. No Geneva convention for you.

Roxanne shook her head. "The nurses would notice if he was depriving his patients. We would talk. And his counts would be off. I never heard anyone say anything bad about Dr. Burns since he came here from UC eight months ago."

"Eight months ago," I repeated. "That's pretty recent." Especially for someone eyeballing retirement. "How long do you think he worked at University College?"

"Someone said he was there his whole career."

"Huh." Many people love St. Joe's, but it ranks maybe fifth tier for academic hospitals and prestige. Patients might ignore the broken equipment and peeling paint, but you come here to get your blood pressure under control or to deliver a baby, not for a cardiac transplant. Family doctors run St. Joe's with a sprinkling of internal medicine, OB/gyn, psychiatry, general surgery, and pediatrics. No trauma. No neurosurgery. Residents head to other hospitals for subspecialty training.

"I wonder why he came here," I said.

"He wanted a change for the worse?" Roxanne grinned at me.

"He definitely got that today." I frowned. "What about Dr. Vrac? Is he from St. Joe's?"

She cackled a laugh. "He showed up maybe three weeks ago when one of our surgeons had an MI."

Myocardial infarction, or heart attack. Dang. "He showed up? From where?"

"UC."

Another academic physician trading down in a short period of time, from the same hospital. "Why?"

"No one knows. But the nurses hate him already."

"Yep." I couldn't say more. Anyone could overhear me and tattle to Vrac. "Keep me posted, okay?"

"I will, *chiquita.*"

I headed for the appendix patient. Slam dunk diagnosis. Typical pain in the right lower quadrant, yelled when I pressed on both the right and the left side of the abdomen and flexed his hip, refused to get out of bed to jump up and down for me. The patient was a guy, so Vrac wouldn't complain that the pain might be his ovaries. Most important of all, the CT ring of truth showed a swollen appendix.

I'd nearly finished dictating the chart when Roxanne whispered in my ear, "They think it was attempted murder."

7

OCTOBER 15, 18:33

GORDON

A medical student with black curls and a bushy beard, his white coat pockets weighed down with a pocket guide and a reflex hammer, stopped by Gordon's cafeteria table. "Hey, I'm Caleb Blau, fourth year." Caleb balanced his brown plastic tray so that his hard-boiled egg didn't roll off.

"Gordon Cole, anesthesia R1." Gordon moved his milk carton back onto his tray, grateful for the company.

Caleb dropped into the plastic chair next to him and rapped his egg on the tray edge, cracking it neatly in two. "I heard what went down in OR 3."

Gordon nodded. Everyone had heard about Joan Finn. He usually ate alone now, as if death were contagious.

"I wanted to tell you what one of my preceptors said. You gotta be ready for it."

"For what?" Milk churned in Gordon's stomach.

Caleb peeled the egg without breaking eye contact. "For them to blame you. You've never been named in a lawsuit before, right?"

Gordon shook his head and then knocked on his temple for good luck.

Caleb bit off the top of the egg, beheading it. "My preceptor said it depends on luck. If the patient or family needs money, who're they gonna go after?"

"Me?" Gordon pressed his knuckles to his mouth.

"He said the hospital'll protect the nurses. Dr. Burns will hire the best lawyer, or his wife will. You were the one keeping the patient stable. The university will only back you up to a certain point. Boom, you're the scapegoat."

"I'm n-n-ot." The fluorescent cafeteria lights burned Gordon's eyes. "The s-s-surgeon wouldn't deflate the abdomen. S-she p-probably d-died of a CO2 embolus. I didn't inject her with CO2."

"Hmmmm. She had a foramen ovale?"

Gordon shook his head. "That would give her a stroke anyway, not cardiovascular collapse."

Caleb waved that away. "Your lawyer will get the autopsy reports. But if you're going head to head with Dr. Vrac—"

Gordon swallowed, or tried to. His mouth had dried out, leaving only a thin coating of mustard.

"Then I feel sorry for you, because he's the nastiest bastard I've never met." Caleb grinned. "And I've worked with surgeons before."

Gordon couldn't laugh. He avoided confrontation, but he had to save his medical career. His parents worked full-time to help with his tuition. If Gordon lost a lawsuit before he'd even finished his training, who would hire him? What hospital would take on that liability? "My lawyer didn't say anything like that."

Caleb pressed his fist against the egg shell bits, crushing them into the tray. "Your lawyer's from the CMPA, right?"

"The one they assigned me, yes." The lawyer, Jun Zhang, had told him to write down all the details of the case and sit tight. No one had filed a lawsuit yet.

Caleb sipped his coffee. "My preceptor said those guys are pretty useless. You want a good one, hire one privately."

"I don't have the money." Gordon tried to keep his line of credit under $300,000.

Caleb laughed. "Me neither. That's what banks are for. Think of it like an investment. You gotta make sure that this doesn't turn against you, or ... " Caleb shrugged and burped, belatedly covering his mouth with his hand.

"I'll do it," said Gordon.

8

MAY 22, 10:44

HOPE

"Dr. Burns?" I mouthed.

Roxanne nodded.

I followed her to the ER lounge, a tiny room that barely fits a short couch, but does boast a microwave, fridge, and coffee maker.

An older nurse, Cathleen, played with her phone on the couch while Roxanne murmured the details to me. "They found a puncture wound in his deltoid."

"Which one?"

She frowned at me. "Didn't say."

I itched to go check his arm for myself. "But they definitely saw the puncture?"

"Yep." Her dark eyes sparkled. "A hole through his scrub sleeve and into his skin. Someone jabbed him straight through his clothes. His tox screen came back positive for narcotics, but they sent blood and tissue samples off for everything, including Sux and Rocuronium, because Dr. Burns didn't respond to the Narcan at all."

"That's true. Not even IV push doses." Narcan, or naloxone, works to counteract narcotics like Fentanyl. When it works, the person can go from comatose to rising from the table like Frankenstein.

It's hard to test for the paralytics Succinylcholine (Sux) and Rocuronium (Roc), and part of me didn't want to picture someone deliberately paralyzing Dr. Burns. I shook my head, trying to keep my voice down while Cathleen, the other nurse, pointedly paid attention. "It could have been an injection of benzos or insulin. We're making a big jump to paralytics."

Cathleen cut in. "They're anesthetists. Everything is about Sux and Roc."

That made me laugh and cringe at the same time. It's true that anesthetists paralyze people more than anyone. We can't have patients moving around as we cut them open.

But paralytics would make a terrifying weapon. I tried to imagine myself unable to breathe, unable to blink, crashing to the ground, knowing that someone had killed me but powerless to scream.

"And they don't think he accidentally injected himself?" I asked, thinking aloud. "Although it's a bit awkward to stab yourself in the deltoid. The quadriceps would be so much easier."

Roxanne crossed her arms. "Forget that, I want to ask you one thing. Where's the syringe?"

We stared at each other while I scoured my brain, sifting through my memory of finding Dr. Burns.

"There wasn't one," I said. "Nothing on the floor, not even after we lifted him up on the gurney."

"I heard the police took his clothes," Cathleen cut in. "They should have found a syringe, ampoules, something."

"Plus they examined the area afterward," said Roxanne. "They didn't find a thing. No syringe. No needle. Nothing except the hole in his arm."

I tried to remember how many people had converged on us. "It was pretty chaotic. Someone could have picked a syringe up afterward without me seeing."

"Yeah, but he couldn't have injected himself and thrown away the syringe when he was overdosed on Fentanyl and/or paralyzed. The killer took all that away."

9

MAY 22, 10:49

HOPE

"This is crazy," said Cathleen, eyes a-glow, already texting.

I couldn't speak. Who would dare try to kill Dr. Burns at the beginning of his work day?

We all knew. Vrac.

Another nurse stuck her head in the room, and Cathleen met her with, "You'll never guess. C'mere."

I mentally replayed the scene again, searching for a plastic syringe. I'd glanced at the floor because I didn't want to trip on anything, so I did have a mental image of blank space in front of the door. I'd helped raise his unconscious body on the gurney and nothing had rolled out from beneath him.

I shook my head. "I definitely didn't see a syringe. Are there any surveillance cameras that we could check? I know it's a long shot for the storage rooms." And for St. Joe's.

"No." Roxanne bit back a laugh. "There are cameras at the hospital's front doors, and they might have rigged something up at the OR entrance, but nothing in the ORs themselves, let alone the storage rooms. Patients are naked. They're not giving consent to be filmed."

"Fair." I wouldn't want cameras filming me naked on an OR table, although video or even audio recording in OR 3 would have stopped

Dr. Vrac a long time ago. "Okay. So there are no cameras in 'stores.' What are these supply rooms for, anyway? I found Dr. Burns in this little side room, almost a closet."

"Those side rooms hold things we don't need to access all the time. My brother-in-law's mesh was kept in there." Roxanne pointed at her groin. "Says it's pretty comfy."

"Oh, you mean he got surgical mesh for a hernia?"

"Yes, but the special kind. The $20,000 kind. Urology keeps their gold clips there too. That sort of thing."

Ah. A glorified storage closet. Open the door, grab the super-expensive equipment, and get out. Unlocked door because Canada trusts everyone, and what the hell, it's a public health system. If someone steals, our taxes go up, but it doesn't feel as personal as a knife to your throat.

"So anyone could get in," I said. "Dr. Burns grabbed something from that closet, someone followed him in, and ... stabby stab stab."

Roxanne cracked a grin."I think just one stab, but yeah."

I checked my watch. "I'll see if I can visit him in the ICU, check the puncture wound, and talk to the staff."

"His attending is Dr. Madeleine Rice. You'll like her." Roxanne frowned. "Busy day today. One of your colleagues is here."

I shook my head in confusion. Residents run the ER. Old news.

Then Roxanne left the lounge with a troubled face, nodding at the chart rack of patients to be seen, and I realized she didn't mean one of us had come to do a consult. One of us had become an emergency room patient.

10

NOVEMBER 4, 15:53

GORDON

"Hanging in there?" Dr. Burns pulled his bright yellow lunch bag out of the lounge fridge.

Gordon shook his head. He hadn't worked with Dr. Burns since that day in September, with Joan Finn. The anesthesiologist must have asked not to have Gordon assigned to him anymore. That hurt.

"You'll be all right," said Dr. Burns, pulling an apple out of the lunch bag. He or his wife had Sharpied R. BURNS on the canvas side. "Have you tried talking to someone?"

"Yes, the lawyer."

Dr. Burns rinsed his apple under the sink before polishing it carefully with a paper towel. "I mean a therapist. My wife suggested I talk to one, and she helped me figure out a few things."

"What do you mean?"

"Don't swim with the sharks." Dr. Burns took another bite from his apple and folded his lunch bag before lowering his voice. "Don't trust the surgeons any farther than you can throw them."

"I know."

"No, it's more than that." Dr. Burns hesitated before he stuck the lunch bag under his arm. "You have to watch out for them, that's all."

11

MAY 22, 10:53

HOPE

I licked my lips and averted my eyes from my classmate's chart. Don't look at charts not assigned to you. Basic medical privacy. So who had gotten sick?

You okay? I texted Tucker first.

He didn't answer. Maddening but understandable during the work day. Could someone have hurt my ex? I quickly added, *I heard one of us ended up in the ER. Is it you?*

Next I messaged Tori Yamamoto, my best friend in residency, who replied, *Not me.*

Tucker wrote, *Mireille's in ER. Can you take a look? They'll put in a surgical consult.* Meanwhile Tori texted, *Mireille.*

Mireille Laroque, the strong, angry resident who wanted general surgery but had matched to family medicine. Mireille wouldn't welcome me poking around her case. I typed back, *I'll have to wait for the consult.*

My phone buzzed with Tucker's irritated response. *Are you in emerg? Just ask her if she wants a friend.*

"She's in bed 10," said Roxanne, passing by and reading my mind.

All righty then. I headed to bed 10 on the acute side, which is close to both the nursing station and the lounge. I'd walked right by her before. I called from behind the drawn curtains, "Mireille?" A pretty name pronounced Meer-*raye*. "It's Hope Sze."

"Oui," came her gruff voice.

I pulled back the curtain, and my mouth dropped open. Mireille was a competitive swimmer who loved medical missions overseas or to Canadian reserves. Always in top shape and in control. I hardly recognized her scraped and swollen face, or her hunched posture with a blanket swaddled around her shoulders. Blood matted the brown curls at her left temple.

A bad feeling surged in my chest, kicking up my heart rate and making me glance over my shoulder while I yanked the curtain closed behind us. "What happened?"

"I don't remember," she said. "I biked to the hospital to work out before I started rounding at 8. I remember that." She started to scratch her head, felt the clotted blood, and dropped her hand back down to her side.

"You fell off your bike? Were you wearing a helmet?"

Contempt crossed her face. "Of course." She glanced around the small room. "Did you take it? I got my crash sensor, my mirror—"

"No, absolutely not. Haven't seen it." I couldn't miss her space age baby blue helmet. She used to lock the helmet to her bike and roll both of them inside the building to lock up because they were so expensive.

"It's important. I want my helmet. I want my bike." She frowned and rubbed her forehead.

Crap. Concussion patients sometimes don't remember their head injury, which is no fun, but did Mireille have a brain bleed? "What do you remember?"

"My kale smoothie breakfast."

Ugh. "Okay. And you remember biking here?"

"Early to work out at the hospital gym before my clinic." She frowned. "I have to meet someone at lunch."

"Okay, don't worry about that. Let's take care of you first."

Mireille scowled so fearsomely that I backed away from her,

bumping into the curtain, before she snapped, "It's important. You have to tell him. What time is it?"

I checked my watch. "10:59."

"I still have time to tell him. We're meeting for lunch."

"So tell him."

"I lost my phone, and I don't remember who it is!"

Right. Her phone must have launched when she flew off her bike. Plus she shouldn't look at her phone if she had a concussion. Screen time in the first 24 hours delays your healing. "I can lend you my phone if you want to log into the cloud."

She screwed up her face. "I can't remember my password, and I didn't write down his name. It's supposed to be a secret. We were texting each other, trying to find a time. He's coming here ... "

I wanted to ask about the head injury, but I played along. "Okay. You're definitely meeting a male, right?"

"Ri-ight." Uncertainty broke her voice.

"Let's say it's a guy for now. One of us can meet him for you if you know when and where. Maybe at the front doors, with the fish tank?" I'd have to run the surgical ward, but someone from our band of residents would get 'er done.

She slowly shook her head. "He wouldn't meet in the hospital. I had to go outside."

"Outside the front doors of the main hospital? Or the FMC?" They set up the Family Medicine Clinic, or FMC, in a separate brick building behind the main hospital. "The subway station's not far from the parking lot around the FMC ... "

Her face tightened. "That's it!"

"The subway station?"

She blinked, but whatever memory had already faded. "Why can't I remember anything?"

"You had a bad fall. Your memory could come back later."

"Or I could have lost it forever," she snapped.

I changed tacks. "Let's walk it back. What time did you leave your apartment?" I'd subletted an apartment in her building on a hill overlooking the Notre-dame-des-Neiges cemetery. She could easily have crashed on her way down the hill.

"Five forty-five. I announced it on Twitter for my exercise accountability group. Sometimes I livestream my rides."

Leaving before dawn seemed unnecessarily self-punitive to me, which explains my matchstick arms and why I'll probably develop osteoporosis before I'm 60. "Okay. And what's the last thing you remember?"

"I latched my helmet good. Then I climbed on my bicycle and set off."

"You remember going down the hill?"

She shook her head. "I remember waking up here."

"In the ER?"

She grimaced. "I remember this stretcher."

"So there's a blank space between your apartment and the ER?"

I could tell it pained her to nod. So 5:45 departure, a ten or fifteen minute bike ride, and then what? "What time did you get to the ER?"

"What?" Mireille put her hand to her head.

"Did you look at the time after your memory came back?"

She shook her head and flinched.

"Your head hurts, eh? Did you get something for the pain?"

She shrugged.

"Okay. Are they doing a CT head?"

She nodded and reached for an empty vomit bag on the bed, holding the cardboard-lined opening up to her mouth.

"Uh, do you know how many times you've vomited?" Medically, we get excited after three pukes. She could have tossed previous bags.

Mireille began to retch. A worrisome sign for a head injury, because it can signify raised intracranial pressure. The torn artery or vein expels more and more blood that presses against the hard confines of the skull.

The person screams with pain, vomits repeatedly, goes unconscious, and dies when the brain herniates through the foramen magnum, the hole meant for the spinal cord.

12

MAY 22, 11:05

HOPE

I busted out of there to find whichever doctor was looking after Mireille. I could still hear her gargling behind me.

"Dr. Soudry," Roxanne told me, correctly reading my crazed expression.

I'd never heard of Dr. Soudry, but I said, "Mireille needs some ondansetron and a head CT."

"Already ordered the CT," said Roxanne, shaking her head. "They should come get her in the next hour or two."

Ugh. Waiting is the name of the medical game in Montreal. "Maybe we could add Gravol and Maxeran and Stemetil," I said.

"Maybe *you* should talk to Dr. Soudry. He's in the lounge."

I got her point. Neither of us were Mireille's attending physician. I checked my still-silent pager and figured I had a few minutes to convince Dr. Soudry, a cheerful, brown-skinned guy sitting on the couch in the miniature lounge where Roxanne and I had whispered earlier.

"Welcome! I've heard of you. Were you the resident who found Mireille?" asked Dr. Soudry.

"No. Who was that?"

"My mistake." He waved a small, white rectangular plasticized bag. "It's coffee," he added, at my confused look. "I'm measuring out the beans before I grind them fresh. Would you like some?"

"No, thanks, I don't drink coffee." I'd also never met an ER doctor who had the time to measure out his beans, but whatever, as long as he could multitask. I quickly updated him about Mireille.

"I can order Maxeran and Stemetil. No problem." He measured his beans out on a portable stainless steel scale as he spoke.

"Do you know what happened to her?"

"No, someone found her in front of the hospital, speaking nonsense."

"What was she saying? Did she explain what happened?"

Dr. Soudry shook his head. "She was speaking in French, as I understand. I don't speak French."

"Right." He looked Middle Eastern. The Quebec government loves taking overseas residents to help take call in our hospitals, even though many of them don't speak French. It was unusual that Dr. Soudry had stayed in Canada to work as staff instead of returning to his country of origin. "Did she have her helmet or bike when she came in?"

"No. I don't know if her helmet was knocked off or if she forgot to wear one."

"She'd wear a baby blue one with all the trimmings, Kevlar, cross-ventilation, a camera, the whole bit." Once Mireille bored me with an in-depth helmet ad. She loved to swim and bike and had been a surgical gunner before detouring to family medicine July 1st.

Now she was a woman with a head injury.

"Don't worry, I'll take good care of her," he said.

"I'm sure," I said. If he put a tenth of attention into Mireille as he did that coffee, she'd benefit. "So you don't know if a car hit her, or if she fell off ... "

"She did say something in English. 'Beam me up, Scotty!'"

I frowned at him. "What?"

"I had to ask about that myself. It's from Star Trek."

"I know it's from Star Trek. It's also a Nicki Minaj album."

"What?" His turn to stare at me. "I can't believe I missed that."

"It's a reissue of her mixtape." I only knew that through Tucker. He memorizes random facts and spews them out non-stop. Never play Trivial Pursuit with him. "I'm more of a Star Wars gal myself, but I've never heard Mireille talk about Star anything before." You know stroke case studies where the patient starts speaking a different language? Maybe she could turn into a Spock fan.

Dr. Soudry shrugged. "Is there anything else I can do to help you and Dr. Laroque?"

I gave him a pained smile. "No. Unless you can speed up the CT."

"I'm trying. We're not a trauma hospital. The technician didn't seem to understand the urgency, so I left a message for the radiologist to call me back."

"I'll go up to radiology to plead her case, if you don't mind."

"Please."

The fact that he hadn't succeeded showed how the Quebec health care system had frayed. Mireille was a resident doctor here. Dr. Soudry had advocated for a swift scan as her attending physician. But she still had to wait hours to see if her brain had been compromised.

13

NOVEMBER 6, 06:50

GORDON

Gordon bounced up and down on his toes, staring out the window at the Montreal skyline, especially the exhaust billowing out of a nearby chimney.

He'd arrived early today and skipped teaching rounds. He had to speak to Dr. Burns.

Surgeons unlocked the doctors' lounge door to grab coffee and joke with each other. One of them read the newspaper while toasting a bagel.

Two anesthesiologists hurried in and out, nodding at Gordon in passing.

Gordon missed the little anesthesia lounge from three years ago. There were never enough chairs, and it smelled like leftovers, but they'd had their own space before renovations forced surgery and anesthesia to merge lounges.

At last, Dr. Burns threw open the door, his hair wet with snow.

"Good morning, Dr. Burns!"

Dr. Burns clutched his yellow lunch bag and stared at Gordon. Then he nodded and crossed the room to place his bag in the fridge.

Gordon fell into step with him on the way out.

"I've got an early case," Dr. Burns muttered.

"This will only take a minute." Gordon followed him into OR 4, where Dr. Burns began checking cables.

"I have another resident today."

"I know that. I needed to talk to you about September 14th."

The breath hissed out of Dr. Burns's mouth. "I have nothing to say."

"'Watch out for them,'" Gordon quoted back to him. "You had to leave the OR on September 14th. You had trouble that entire week. I notice you always bring your lunch."

Dr. Burns frowned as he turned on the gas analyzer. "What of it?"

"Your yellow lunch bag has your name on the side."

The ghost of a smile touched Dr. Burns's lips while he uncapped a syringe and drew up some Rocuronium. "My wife marked my bag so no one would steal her excellent food. You know how that happens."

"It does, but it's such a distinctive bag, and people go in and out of the lounge all the time."

"What are you saying?" Dr. Burns capped the syringe and placed it on his cart.

"Could someone have put something in your food or drink?"

"My food ..." Now Dr. Burns placed both hands on the cart.

Gordon looked away, but Dr. Vrac's gleeful voice echoed in his head and probably in his supervisor's as well.

Stinks in here.

Someone's got a bad case of the farts today.

"We all prescribe Gogolax," said Gordon. "It's tasteless and odorless. You can mix it with water."

"A few times I've wondered about the texture of my food," said Dr. Burns. "I thought Nikki was busy, or hadn't washed the dishes quite right." He pressed a hand to his head. "You think he—"

"He might've meant it as a joke," said Gordon. "Is it still happening?"

Dr. Burns's face reddened as he swore and admitted, "It's not as severe."

"Your body might be adapting."

"He's probably not poisoning me now since I refuse to work with him, but he could be." Dr. Burns stared at the ceiling. "It would explain why I had to run out that day."

"That's why I had to tell you."

Dr. Burns started to reach for Gordon, then stopped himself. "Thank you." He pulled his phone out of his pocket. "I must speak to my lawyer. I have no proof, of course."

"Maybe we could tempt him into doing it again."

Dr. Burns paused, phone in hand. "What do you mean?"

"We could set up a camera in the fridge. Then, when he tampered with your food, you'd have evidence. We could send the food and drink away for testing."

"It's a risky proposition. I don't know the legalities of filming without people's consent."

It wasn't a no. Gordon waited.

At last, Dr. Burns said, "If you want to do it, I won't stop you."

14

MAY 22, 11:21

HOPE

I managed to convince radiology to scan Mireille once I tracked down the doctor in charge of CTs, an affable grey-haired guy wearing plaid.

"Oh, I know who you mean," he said. He'd planted his potbelly squarely in front of three different screens in his darkened room. He'd drawn his window shades to view the images. "When she was on general surgery last year, she used to bug me to read her scans first."

"Exactly."

"She's in family medicine now?"

"Yep. A bad bike accident this morning knocked her helmet off. Possible loss of consciousness. Headache. Amnesia. Started vomiting in front of me."

He frowned. "She should be at a trauma hospital."

"I know. But she's here now and needs a CT head. Could you help her?"

"Of course. I don't know why her attending didn't call."

"I hear he did, but ... " I shrugged, changed the subject by thanking him profusely, and called Cheng as soon as I left radiology. The lack of sunlight in that wing depressed me. "Hey, I finished the consult. It's an appy." Infected appendix.

"Great, I'll check him out and put him on the board. How's Robert Burns?"

Dr. Burns. "In ICU?"

"Yeah. I'm stuck on the floor"—the surgical ward—"but all of us are wondering how he's doing, and you were the one who saved him."

"Team effort," I said.

"Singh wants to know too. I'll cover ER and the floor to give you time."

"Amazing, thanks." Unbelievably nice of him. I smiled until, on the stairs, I realized that Vrac might be leaning on them to figure out if his enemy had died. Cheng also hadn't explained the ghost rumors. Sigh.

I located the small, seven bed ICU on the third floor beside a tiny CCU and a seven bed step-down unit. The ICU's automatic door slid open when I beeped my badge.

"So you're the one who found Bob Burns," said a round woman with Asiatic eyes and dark brown skin contrasting with her white lab coat.

The coat could mean she was a doctor, but the clerks in the ER also wear white coats, so I quickly read her badge and determined that yep, the ICU physician, Dr. Rice, stood before me.

"Yes, hello, Dr. Rice. I'm Dr. Hope Sze, the resident on general surgery. Would it be possible to see him?"

"Definitely," she said. I liked her short lion's mane of curly blondish brown hair, cobalt shirt, and red jeans. "Heard you ran a good code and you're applying to the emergency medicine program."

"Thanks so much. We did have a good team." Blood roasted my cheeks. Other classmates excelled at kissing ass and taking credit for other people's work. I struggled to accept a compliment, but needed to impress this doctor to win a spot in the somewhat vicious competition for a year-long ER specialization program after my family medicine residency.

Dr. Rice pointed to a bed in the far left corner. "His wife would like to speak to you. I'd stay longer, but my resident is indisposed." She checked her watch.

"Who's your resident?" I couldn't help asking.

"Dr. Laroque."

Mireille was doing ICU! My eyebrows jumped.

Dr. Rice nodded in approval. "We asked for volunteers to rotate through the ICU early. A few eager first years took us up on the offer."

"I'm one of them," I said.

"Yes, I saw you on the schedule." Her smile widened.

Dr. Rice knew everything, and Mireille had biked in at 05:45 before ICU rounds. Powerhouses all around me as I made my way to Dr. and Mrs. Burns.

Dr. Burns was intubated, sedated, hooked up to the cardiac monitor, and had multiple IVs running. His numbers looked good. His colour had improved. The ICU nurse and I nodded at each other before I held out my hand to Mrs. Burns, a short, white brunette with spiky highlights and precise makeup. She looked ready for brunch with her girlfriends, not "the unit," or ICU.

"Hello, I'm Dr. Hope Sze," I said awkwardly. "I'm the junior resident on general surgery this month."

"Nikki Burns. You found my husband," she said. "He would have died."

I opened my mouth because someone else might have found him. Then I closed it because every second counts in a code. Time is brain.

Nikki's arched eyebrows rose. "Someone tried to kill him. I knew that even before I found the mark in his sleeve and in his arm."

Puncture wound confirmed. I bit my lip.

Nikki didn't hesitate. "There was no syringe on the floor, right?"

I nodded. "No syringe that I saw."

A smile slashed across Nikki's face. "So it was attempted murder. Dr. Vrac will say he's a drug addict and that all anesthesiologists are on drugs, but Bob never abused a single ampoule."

I flinched.

"I knew it. Dr. Vrac. Am I right?"

While we ran the code on your husband, I thought, but couldn't say.

"You should remember that less than 10 percent of doctors are addicted to drugs. My Bob was one of the 90 percent."

"I understand," I said.

"His sister got addicted to prescription drugs. He was passionate about saving anyone else from that."

I made a sad face. "Is she okay?"

"Yes, she works for addiction services as a counsellor out west, and she has a beautiful family of her own. Ask her. Ask her about Bob."

I nodded, even though I had no contact information for her.

"I know you, Hope Sze. I know what you're capable of." Her eyes bored into mine as if she could read my mind and transcribe my thoughts. "I want you to find out the truth and tell the world." She waved her hand at the bed where her husband lay. "Protect his name. I'll pay you to find out everything you can."

I held up my hands, trying to ward off her intensity. "I'm not a real detective. I can't accept any money."

"But it takes time and expertise to ask the right questions from the right people. I can't do that, but I've got the money." Her whitened teeth gleamed in stark contrast to her clothes. She wore all black already, as if Dr. Burns had died.

"Wouldn't you like a real private investigator instead?" I asked.

"I've hired PI Jefferson Hollingsworth, in addition to my lawyer and the police." She showed me her phone, although I didn't recognize the private investigator's name. "Don't worry, you won't be alone. We'll figure this out faster with more expertise. So will you help us?"

"How about this. I'll let you know if I find anything out, and we can talk then." My heart thumped in embarrassment. It felt weird mentioning money over Dr. Burns's unconscious body. I couldn't afford to bankrupt myself on a possible fool's errand, but I could ask some questions.

"Absolutely. I'm a businesswoman myself. I know how little residents make and how high tuition is. I'm happy to compensate you for your time."

I touched the table beside her hand. Most people don't know, or care, that residents can run up to half a million dollars in debt before we start earning a living. "If you're comfortable, please tell me about your husband and who you think might have hurt him."

"Vladimir Vrac," she said immediately. "He hated my husband."

My thoughts exactly, although I hadn't known his first name. I exhaled and glanced at her husband's monitor. Blood pressure 130/95, heart rate 89, no expression showing that he could hear or understand us.

"We can go to the family room," she said. "I'll sign a paper so that you can look at Bob's chart as part of his circle of care. They already documented that puncture wound in his arm."

Wow. She ran an investigation on steroids.

"As a doctor, and part of the surgical team, you'll hear things a regular PI won't. I need boots on the ground. Let's go somewhere to talk."

I couldn't argue with her. She was like a human forcefield. She kissed her husband on the cheek and pointed me back toward the entrance. I'd walked right by a tiny family room crammed with furniture. No window, but they'd hung a print of a seaside village on the wall opposite the door.

"Here." Mrs. Burns gestured at the burgundy couch and sank into the love seat beside it. "Want a coffee? They have those pods."

"No, thanks." Even if I drank coffee, plastic pods hurt the environment. I perched on the couch.

"Me neither. Screw coffee when your husband is dying, right?" She ran her hand through her short hair.

My throat ached, and I wished I could drink some water. "He's stable. It's a good sign."

Her eyes narrowed, not arguing but not buying it. "He needs UC Hospital as soon as a bed opens up. Now tell me exactly what happened." She pulled out her phone and pressed the voice memo button. "I assume you don't mind me recording this."

Uh oh. "You can record it, but I'll need to get back to surgery soon."

She waved her hand. "Bob waited for surgeons his entire life. You know they want the patient and anesthesia in the room stat and then half the time, they don't show up on time themselves? I was an OR nurse and then a charge nurse at UC. I know what I'm talking about."

"That must be so frustrating, but I know a lot of punctual surgeons." Not me. I rush to clinic at the last second.

She cackled a laugh. "#notallsurgeons, right? I get it. You'll go hail Vlad the Impaler."

I flinched. For a near-widow, she seemed ...

"Too honest, right? People have said that my whole life." Her eyes suddenly filled with tears. "Bob liked it, though. That's why we made a good match. He was so quiet most of the time, while I called out all the BS—and believe me, there was a lot."

"I believe it." Bull galore.

"Vrac was the worst. The ultimate bully. We'd wait while he read the newspaper and drank coffee in the lounge. He'd send his residents in, but scream if they dared cut the skin before he toddled in. If you didn't bow low enough when he arrived, he'd show up even later the next time."

I could totally picture this.

"I called Vrac on it. The OR charge nurse is like air traffic control. For every OR, we know which surgeon's doing which procedure with which anesthesiologist and which nurses, what time they're in or out, who's fast, who's slow. We run it all. If they're late, we cancel the last case. They called me Nikki the Nag, Nasty Nik, whatever. They hated me even worse than Tammy, the charge nurse who worked there for a dog's age and still fills in at UC once in a while. I didn't care. I told Vladdy, I'm not here to make friends. I'm here to make the ORs run on time."

So many questions. "And you think Dr. Vrac held a grudge against Dr. Burns?"

"Of course. Bob's a teddy bear. He's no match for that b—" She glanced toward his bed in the unit and cut the swear word off. "Especially now."

"So you think Dr. Vrac might have stabbed Dr. Burns with a needle this morning?"

She nodded. "It's been brewing a long time. Bob tried not to get scheduled with Vlad the Impaler, but he didn't always have a choice. When he switched hospitals, Vlad followed him."

"So Dr. Vrac and Dr. Burns used to work together at UC?" I double-checked Roxanne's intel.

Nikki stared at me with pity. "You're not up on the gossip, are you? Did you not go to McGill for medical school?"

"Western."

She sighed. "Bob and Vlad and I used to work together at UC. University College Hospital." She felt the need to spell it out for me. "The trauma hospital. The big guns. Bob's an academic and loved it there, but he couldn't stand the demon of OR 3, and the powers that be didn't approve of our relationship. He transferred to St. Joe's."

I nodded. Although doctors and nurses get together, it's a bit more frowned upon nowadays.

"Last month, Vlad transferred here too, making a scene, demanding OR 3 because that's his lucky number, even though people here talk about a 'presence' in that OR."

The ghost rumors, confirmed by someone else! Not the right time to ask, but the tips of my fingers tingled.

Nikki shrugged. "I told Bob we couldn't keep running. I asked scheduling to keep them apart because of the lawsuit."

I held up my palm. "Lawsuit?"

She sighed. "You don't know about that either."

"No, ma'am."

"Call me Nikki. Ma'am makes me want to break out the Botox." She touched her forehead reflexively before she continued softly, "Anyway, both of them were named in a lawsuit regarding a patient named Joan Finn. We don't speak of it."

We don't speak about lawsuits. Like the song "We Don't Talk About Bruno," only less catchy. "I'll need the details on that in case it's relevant."

"Good idea. I'll send you the documents I can dig up. You can also ask your senior resident."

I blinked at her.

"He was named too. I saw his name in Bob's chart. Raj Singh, right? He was operating the day Joan Finn died."

15

MAY 22, 11:43

HOPE

My head spun as I made my way to the surgeons' lounge on the fourth floor, trying not to bump into OR staff who checked their phones.

"Hope!" Mike Cheng tried to hand me a coffee.

"No, thanks. You go ahead." Instead, I sipped water and admired the sunlight streaming through the large windows. I wouldn't leave the hospital for up to 36 hours on call.

Cheng took a big gulp. "I'll get you something later. You got an update for us?"

"Dr. Burns is stable in ICU. His wife wants to move him to UC, but they have no beds right now."

"He definitely needs UC," said Cheng. "Plus Nikki wants to know who stabbed him with a syringe, right?"

Word travels fast. "She has a theory."

"Vlad the Impaler."

"Yep."

Cheng grinned at me over his coffee cup. "He goes by Vance here, by the way. Says we 'morons' pronounce Vlad wrong, but Vladimir is on all his certificates."

"Right." I wouldn't call Dr. Vrac by his first name. "Where is he, anyway?"

Cheng lowered his voice. "Last I saw him, he was yelling about his car. 'Do mine first!' He hung up to put the moves on a student nurse. 'I can help you with anatomy.'"

He imitated Vrac's thin, creepy voice, breaking out the goose-bumps on my arms. I shivered and changed the subject. "Are we still operating today?"

Cheng shook his head. "Not unless he steals anesthesia from someone else's room, and good luck with that. But we're on call, everything'll come our way after hours. How's the appendix?"

I explained the case in more detail, and he texted Singh. "It's on the board as a B case."

I nodded. We rank surgeries by urgency, and an appendix only kills you slowly, so it's not an A case. "He's on Ceftriaxone and Flagyl, and I increased his morphine a bit. He's been NPO since last night." Nil per os, so no eating and drinking until post-op, poor guy, but at least he got antibiotics and pain control.

"Yeah, we'll get him done. You want to scrub in?"

"For sure. As long as there's room."

"Aww, I think we can make room for the conquering hero." He winked at me.

My face reddened. Post-Tucker, I'd sworn off all men, women, and non-binary people, but I couldn't help noticing Cheng. Yikes.

He clapped me on the back. "Now tell me what happened."

I nodded. "And you'll catch me up with what you did today, okay?"

"You want to know my alibi." His dark eyes glinted with amusement. "Don't worry, I've got one. I was right in this room in between cases. And so was Dr. Vrac."

16

MAY 22, 11:46

HOPE

"Hold up." I literally held my hand in the air. "You're telling me that Dr. Vrac was *here*, in this lounge, when Dr. Burns disappeared? Before the second case, Dr. Vrac yelled at us in the OR, then you said you'd find Dr. Burns."

Cheng nodded. "Yeah, I figured coffee would fortify me while I checked for Burns in the lounge, which was the most logical place for him."

"That's true."

Cheng grinned at me. "I grabbed a cup of joe. No Burns. I was about to give up when Vrac came in."

I frowned. "How long of a lag was that?"

"I didn't check my watch. Maybe seven minutes?" Cheng shrugged. "I see what you're getting at. He could have injected Burns in the time between us leaving him in the OR and him showing up in the lounge. I can't help you there. But my alibi stands. I headed straight from the OR to the lounge. Probably a dozen people saw me."

Excellent alibi, achieved by not helping us find Dr. Burns. Which made me like him a little less. Competitive specialties like urology attract not only smart and lucky applicants, but ones who coast on their charm and take advantage of others when they can get away with it.

"Don't look at me like that." Cheng grinned at me. "I thought Dr. Burns might be in the lounge. He likes to eat. His wife packs him all the best food in a yellow lunch bag with his name on it."

My stomach growled in sympathy. Like most ethnic people, including Dr. Burns, eating is kind of my religion.

Cheng opened the door and pointed at a neat yellow bag at the back. "See? Big enough for a thermos, a lunch, and two snacks."

I eyeballed him. "Did you peek?"

"Nah. I know his eating habits. He's grouchy if anyone touches his stuff. Once Burns accused Vrac of messing with it, and then he didn't use the fridge for a few days, but he gave up after that. Didn't want to schlep ice packs around for his yummies."

"Did Dr. Vrac touch his food?"

"Not that I saw, but Vrac's always in there." He lowered his voice. "Don't leave anything in the fridge if you really want it."

Great. On top of everything else, Vrac stole other people's food. Seriously, the man could not go any lower. "You never saw Dr. Burns come in after our first case today, right?"

"Right. That case ended, I gave you a tour, we tried to start the next case, and I ended up here with Vrac. Next thing I knew, you were hollering for help, and I ran to the code and saw Dr. Burns then."

I read between the lines. Once Dr. Vrac entered the lounge, Cheng could easily have come out to help me and Singh find Dr. Burns. But no sense yelling at the guy. "Yeah, I remember you at the code. You put in a line, right?"

"I can drill all day and all night." He winked at me again.

Eh. Kind of a scoundrel, but a likeable one. "Singh stood at the head of the bed for the code." I calculated my chief's alibi. He'd searched for Dr. Burns, then helped with the code. I didn't think he'd stabbed Dr. Burns.

Which still left me dozens more people in the OR who'd need their alibis checked. I sighed. "Do you know the people who work here? The doctors and nurses? I want to figure out their alibis. Can you help me?"

He thought about it. "I don't have a lot of free time."

"None of us do, but Mrs. Burns asked me."

He raised his eyebrows. "Nikki Burns?"

"You know her?"

"Everyone knows Nikki Burns. She used to run the UC's OR with an iron fist."

I could see that. She was a strong woman. "She mentioned that."

"Yeah. Once she started sleeping with the top dogs, she was unstoppable."

I raised my eyebrows. Never mind Nikki's education and confidence, people always accused women of sleeping their way to the top, setting off my BS meter. "Dr. Burns was the top dog?"

Cheng's eyes flickered. "Never mind. Listen, I don't think I'll be able to help you much."

"Really?" First ghost rumors, now no help with the investigation?

He saw the look on my face and reconsidered, grinning at me. "Except Delilah. I'll question her any day of the week."

17

NOVEMBER 10, 12:45

GORDON

While Gordon waited for his camera to trap someone, he worked, studied, and dreaded Joan Finn's lawyers. Any moment in the hospital, or even his apartment, someone could serve him papers.

To stay sane, Gordon began investigating Dr. Vrac. What did anyone know about the surgeon besides his love of cars and women's behinds?

Gordon strained to remember something useful that might implicate the surgeon. Where had he grown up? Where did he go to school?

"Sprang fully-formed from the head of Zeus," Vrac said once.

Another time: "I don't have family. I hate family."

At the time, the OR staff had laughed uneasily, but even an orphan would have been raised somewhere.

Gordon typed "Dr. Vladimir Vrac" into his search engine.

He scanned the man's archived bios at University College Hospital and McGill University. Dr. Vrac had studied minimally invasive surgery at McGill over 15 years before, about 1.5 times the age of the other fellows. Where had Vrac completed his medical school or residency? Usually they bragged about as many credentials as possible.

Luckily, with a name like Vladimir Vrac, Gordon quickly tracked that the man had graduated from medical school in the Caribbean and slogged through general surgery in Baltimore. Vrac had covered a few different community hospitals across the American eastern seaboard before moving to McGill 16 years ago.

"Interesting," said Gordon softly. The medical establishment looked down on community hospitals and especially International medical graduates, or IMGs. Although IMGs may have received excellent training in China or Ukraine or wherever else, the Canadian system made them redo their exams and sometimes their residencies if they were lucky enough to get a training spot, basically jumping through dozens of expensive hoops until some gave up on practicing medicine and drove taxis.

Did Vrac's animosity stem from his history as an IMG?

Gordon shook his head. Dr. Vrac had leapt through his last hoop in Canada decades ago. His empty bio covered up ancient history. Did the man simply bribe his way in with generous donations to the foundations?

Keep digging, *Gordon told himself.* Keep digging like your life, and your career, depend on it.

18

MAY 22, 11:59

HOPE

The pretty OR nurse, Delilah, stared into the mirror above the bathroom sinks.

"Are you okay?" I asked her.

Her shoulders huddled forward. "I've never been so scared in my life. Dr. Burns almost died."

"Totally normal," I said. "We're all freaked out, right?" They train doctors not to react so that we can keep shovelling through patients, but I think nurses give each other more space to grieve. "I'm Hope Sze, the new junior off-service resident. Do you, ah, have any idea what might have happened to Dr. Burns? Did you see anything?"

She snorted. "I see trocars and laparoscopes and not much else."

"I hear you." Trocars are hollow metal tubes containing a pointy bit so you can cut through the outer layers of flesh, get to the good stuff, and withdraw the pointy bit, leaving a drainage tube. They sometimes make chest tubes packaged with trocars.

Delilah flipped her hair. "All I know is that I didn't try to kill him. Dr. Burns was one of the good ones, okay?"

"Okay."

Her shoulders relaxed. "Lots of the guys are pigs. Not him. He doesn't make me 'ride his Tesla'."

"Mercedes," I said, remembering Vrac's sleazy offer.

"Oh, he has a bazillion cars. Once he started naming them alphabetically. Audi, BMW, Cadillac, DeLorean, an E-something that was a Mercedes. He must've named ten cars." She snorted.

"Did you go for a ride?" I heard the double entendre in my own voice.

"'Course not! He's, like, my *grandfather's* age."

"Yeah." Cheng had volunteered to question Delilah too. Some non-gentlemen did prefer blondes. So did blondes actually have *less* fun? I shrugged. "I hear you. Do you have an alibi for this morning?"

"I just told you that I didn't hurt Dr. Burns!"

I exhaled. "I don't think you injected him, but you know what they say: trust but verify."

Her forehead crinkled. "Who says that?"

"I'd have to look it up. I'm still asking everyone if they have an alibi." She gave me an injured kitten look, and I softened my tone even more. "I'm making a spreadsheet." I showed it to her on my phone. So far, I'd cleared myself and Singh. I might add Cheng and Vrac if someone else testified they'd both been in the lounge for long enough.

The spreadsheet reassured her that it wasn't personal. "Oh, okay. I was in the women's change room. My contact lens was killing me. I had to rinse it out."

"Who else was in the bathroom? Could you add them to my spreadsheet?"

"Sure. But I don't know exactly what time it was, only that it was between cases. I needed the extra time because that contact hurt so much."

I sighed. I couldn't get too precise about alibis. Good thing I didn't do this for a living and the police and private detective would follow everything up.

Delilah took my phone to add names. "Amelia, Sharleen, Wanda, Valentina, and Emily. Someone was already in the stall before me, I don't know who. Black clogs and scrubs, but that could be anybody."

Huh. I made a mental note to check people's feet. Everyone in the

OR wears plastic clogs, the kind of shoe you slip into without a closed heel back, and washable in case of blood or worse.

"I heard you're working for Nikki," Delilah added.

Hospital gossip beats the speed of light. "Do you know Nikki from UC?" I asked. Delilah looked young, but I'd heard you can start working as an RPN before you're 20. You can bounce from hospital to hospital or work simultaneously at a few locations if you want.

Delilah grimaced. "I know Nikki from the Christmas parties. She's kind of extra."

I tilted my head, inviting her to spill the tea, which sounds much nicer than gossip.

"She always drinks too much and ... well, I shouldn't say. But I always wondered why Dr. Burns got together with her. I thought—" She bit her lip.

"You can tell me. I'm not passing on anything that's not relevant."

She shook her head. "I don't want to talk behind anyone's back. I'll get a bad rep."

"Not from me. I don't know anyone to tell. It's my first day in the OR."

"No, thanks. I don't want to get involved. Working here is like living in a goldfish bowl. Someone here noticed that I gained two pounds and asked me if I was pregnant. Two pounds!"

"Rude. Also kind of ridiculous."

"She said it was because it would affect staffing if I had to take maternity leave, but ... "

"People are dicks to women in general. Mat leave is an excuse," I said. Maternity/paternity/parental leave, child care, ailing parents, depression ... the medical system doesn't care about actual health care providers' issues. Show up and work. Work harder.

She nodded and redid her ponytail, drawing out her hair. "I didn't kill anyone, especially not Dr. Burns. And I'm not going to. I just want to do my job. Is that so hard?"

"Sing it, sister," I said.

She laughed and blushed. "I'm talking too much, right?"

I shook my head. "I think you're pretty normal. Hey—"

My phone buzzed. Cheng wrote, *Brace yourself. Vrac's heading.*

Heading where? I quickly wrote back.

"Hey, what?"

"Want to be friends?" I blurted out. "It's kind of a sausage fest here."

She pealed with laughter.

Heading out, Cheng wrote. *He told Singh to cover for him.*

WTF did that mean? Of course the senior resident would cover for him, but what if we got called into an emergency surgery? Could Singh take over the operation legally?

Singh might let me operate a little.

When I tuned back in, Delilah was saying something about the circulating nurse, and how the charge nurse hadn't taken a shine to her.

"It's kind of a bitch fest too. See you later, friend." Delilah dimpled at me, because of course she had dimples, and hustled out of the bathroom.

19

NOVEMBER 10, 13:23

GORDON

The Internet kept directing Gordon to French pages. He learned that "vrac" means bulk in French. Zero waste pages encouraged him to try buying "en vrac."

The unique last name served another purpose. Gordon found evidence of Vladimir Vrac scoring a winning goal at a soccer game at a middle school tournament in Regina, Saskatchewan.

At least the man had told the truth about his age. He was, indeed, 62 years old when Gordon did the math.

The newspaper published a few photos, including one of Vladimir hugging his brother, Mikhail Vrac. A taller figure behind them, her face too pixelated to make out, was identified as their mother, Nadia Smith.

What had happened to Vlad Vrac's family?

20

MAY 22, 12:10

HOPE

I ran into Tori Yamamoto at lunch in the residents' lounge. Hanging out with my home girl almost made me forget the trays abandoned on the table and the drone of a Law and Order rerun on the TV in the background.

Tori grinned at me. Everyone else crammed on the couch, their eyes fixed either to their phones or the TV, except one woman clicking on a desktop in the corner. Tori sat at the round table directly in front of the door, drawing on a piece of paper with a black felt tip pen.

"You heard about Mireille?" I asked, dropping beside Tori after I dug my cream cheese sandwich out of the fridge.

She covered her drawing with her free hand. "Yes, I was the one who found her."

One mystery solved. Dr. Soudry had mistaken me for Tori earlier because we're both Asian female residents. I sighed and rolled with it. "Where did you find her?"

"On Peloquin Street."

That's the main one-way street in front of our hospital where the circular driveway leads to the main gate. On the left side of the hospital is the ambulance/ER entrance. If you keep following that path past the ER side, you'll run into the brick Family Medicine Centre building surrounded by what seems like an acre of parking.

"What was she doing there?"

Tori grimaced and made a tick on her drawing. "Wandering around bruised and confused."

"With her bike?"

Tori shook her head and tapped her pen against her chin. "She was searching for it, calling, 'Bike! Helmet! C'mere, I need you!'"

I pictured Mireille limping along the sidewalk, her curls matted with blood, scouring the bushes for her stuff. "She spoke to you in English?"

"That part was in English. I didn't understand the French so well, but I convinced her to go to the ER with me." Tori added a swoop to her drawing, but covered it with her hand when I peeked.

"Did she say a car hit her, or she fell?"

"She mostly swore at me. I couldn't get much out of her."

That sounded about right.

"When I asked her, she hummed a song I didn't recognize." She hummed it for me now, elegant but lower than her natural pitch.

I shrugged. "I don't know it either. We could Shazam it if you're curious?" I opened my phone's app to identify music.

Tori grinned at me. "I already tried it when I was with her, for something to do, even though I didn't expect it to work with her singing. And it didn't."

I nodded.

"Then Mireille said, 'Young men dead.'"

The skin prickled on my arms. I rubbed them, partly to comfort myself. "Young men *dead?"*

"Exactly. After that, she started vomiting."

"Young men dead," I repeated. "Maybe she was hallucinating?"

Tori shook her head. "She didn't react to anything except me. She didn't seem to see or hear anything else. Her words didn't make a whole lot of sense, though. I don't know."

"That's a great song," piped up a male voice from the sofa.

Both of us gazed in surprise at the medical student I'd met that morning. The one who called OR 3 the death OR.

"Excuse me?" Tori said as she turned her drawing over to hide it completely.

"I'm Gary. Hope and I did psychiatry together, remember?" He grinned at me, and my eyes popped. I did rotate through psychiatry with three medical students, whom I mentally considered Huey, Dewey, and Louie—three nice, clean, mostly harmless med students. I got to know Robert pretty well, but Gary?

"I got a perm," he explained. "I wanted a new look and didn't feel like dyeing it."

"Okay," I said slowly. He did look familiar. Maybe the curly hair had thrown me off. "What song are you talking about?"

"One by The Black Angels. Here, I'll play it for you." He clambered off the edge of the couch, pushing the curls out of his eyes again while he scrolled through his phone. "Here."

Hard to describe the pounding, insistent guitar chords that filled the air. Two people watching TV gestured at us to turn it down.

Gary thumbed down the volume, still smiling. "Good memories."

"Of what?" I asked. "It sounds like it's from the 1970s. Not in a bad way." The kind of music you might listen to on a road trip, or while smoking a bong.

"The Last of Us Part II."

I glanced at Tori, who shook her head.

"It's a video game. This song plays during the finale." He smiled fondly, probably imagining the game. "Anyway, thanks for the memories."

We glanced at each other and silently agreed to escape Gary. I tossed my lunch remains in the fridge.

Tori drank a bit of water before she stowed her bottle and whispered in my ear, "How are you doing after finding Dr. Burns?"

"I'm okay. I wondered ... "

"If I might have some insight?" She grinned at me and wrote **Boo!** on the back of her drawing.

I laughed out loud. Tori doesn't show most people her sly sense of humour. Or anything else. Only after we'd been friends for three quarters of a year did she let her special ability slip, that she can see ghosts.

Yep, ghosts. Not all the time, and not everywhere, but sometimes. Hence, boo.

Tori tacked her drawing to the fridge back to front with a stray magnet. I itched to flip it over and check the drawing, but she slipped out of the lounge, and I had to follow her.

After the resident lounge door closed behind us, Tori murmured, "I don't know Dr. Vrac."

"Right, but what if you met Dr. Burns? Maybe something would ... come up? Nikki Burns gave me carte blanche. I'm sure she'd let me bring you up to the ICU. If you wanted."

I checked my pager. Although St. Joe's gen surg was a baby rotation compared to one at a trauma hospital, you can't count on eating and drinking when you're on call. *You have to decide if you're too hungry to sleep or too tired to eat,* observed one of my classmates. On gen surg in clerkship, I ate "lunch" at 7 p.m. and "supper" at 3 a.m., too hungry to sleep.

I had extra time today because our ORs had been cancelled by what happened to Dr. Burns. #theupsideofattemptedmurder

"Have you ... had any visions?" I asked awkwardly as we clopped down the stairs. Our footsteps echoed on the walls and ceiling. I can't bring up ghosts in a public place.

She shook her head. "I'll let you know. Right now, I need to find Mireille's bike and helmet. She gave me her key, and she's counting on me to get them."

"Okay. But you have no idea where she put them?" Concussions can lead to anterograde amnesia (can't form new memories) or retrograde amnesia (can't remember your retro, or your past). "I'll help you if I don't get paged. Where did you already look?"

Tori frowned. The crummy stair lights cast shadows on her face. "I haven't had a chance between bringing Mireille to the ER and doing clinic."

She led me outside to the bike racks at the front of St. Joe's, where one patient smoked and another yelled on her cell phone. None of the five bikes locked here had been totalled. Ergo, none of them were Mireille's.

Tori pointed behind the hospital. "Let's check by the FMC too."

Because the Family Medicine Centre has its own separate building, it would have been faster to take a back door out of the hospital than to circle around. But no one had paged me yet, so we hurried around the picnic tables, a few more bike racks, and the ambulance parked outside the ER.

From 20 feet away, the bright blue twisted frame of Mireille's bike caught my eye.

Apart from the light clinging to a handlebar, it was totalled. Bent frame, warped tires. Yet Mireille had carefully locked it to the bike rack, along with her baby blue helmet.

"That's strange. She normally would have brought the bike in with her, right? How did she end up locking the bike up here and then wandering down to Peloquin where you found her?"

"No idea," said Tori. She unlocked the bike, clicked the helmet over her arm, and began wheeling the bike with some difficulty.

"Where are you going?" I asked. The bike looked like it should go straight in the trash can.

"Mireille kept asking for this before she gave me the key. I promised her I'd put it somewhere safe, like the residents' lounge."

I nudged the wobbly rear tire to keep it travelling in a more straight line. "Nah. If you want to keep this puppy safe, you'd better lock it up. Want my call room?"

"Sure. Then I can tell her it's locked away. I guess it's expensive. She called it the ultimate biking machine."

No longer, I sighed, but kept that to myself. Even bent like Beckham, the biking machine might provide some comfort to our friend getting a CT scan.

The bike's tires seemed to degrade with every step, rubbing against the frame and slapping the pavement. Then I heard something else.

21

MAY 22, 12:22

HOPE

I stopped still. "Did you hear that?"

"What?" Tori urged the bike on, checking her watch.

"I'm serious." I tuned my ears and did a 360, listening carefully before I pointed toward the main street, Queen Mary, across the parking lot. "That way."

Tori wanted to argue with me, but then she heard it too. "What is it?"

My heart thudded in my chest. "It sounds human."

"And in pain," she said quietly.

We chained the bike back up again. You can't triangulate properly when you're weighed down with a barely-functioning set of wheels.

"Should we call 911?" I asked.

"Once we find the source," she said, but she looked pale, and I remembered that she'd already located Mireille this morning. It made me wonder again what Tori had been sketching. What ghosts did Tori have to exorcise today?

"We're together," I said. "No one can sneak up on us if we stand back to back." I'd seen horses in a field like this, head to nose, peacefully grazing while protecting each other.

"That seems extreme," said Tori, but we pressed side to side, straining our ears.

No more cars entered the parking lot filled with rows upon rows of vehicles. St. Joe's didn't aspire to University College's multi-level parking, where they have valets to take your keys if the lot is too full. Those valets will jockey your car around and you can run to your clinic. St. Joe's only uses the pavement outside its hospital and FMC, and when the lot's full, it's full.

It felt eerily still. Usually one car might leave, or grumpy residents may cut through the parking lot on their way to clinic.

I heard nothing except our breathing and someone moaning softly, in pain, somewhere in this parking lot.

At last, we wove our way toward a figure crumpled between the cars.

"Hello?" I said, too loud, before I saw the blood pooling under his head.

He tried to roll toward me, and I screamed.

22

MAY 22, 12:25

HOPE

Encrusted blood covered half the man's face. The blood had even seeped between his teeth.

Tori calmly pulled out her phone to call for help, which left the hands-on part to me.

I donned the spare set of blue gloves in my back pocket and cautiously approached the man. "I'm Dr. Hope Sze. I'm here to help you."

He groaned again. Then he fell silent while I steadied his head to make sure he didn't aggravate a cervical spine (C-spine, or neck) fracture.

Bleeding head+can't talk=bad news

Another head injury, much worse than Mireille's since he could no longer form words. He could move his right hand, which stirred, zombie-like.

"GCS 1+2+5, or 8," I decided aloud. The Glasgow Coma Scale, or GCS, helps us estimate the patient's degree of brain injury based on their ability to open their eyes, talk, or move. Less than 8, intubate: install a breathing tube so they don't choke.

Tori repeated, "GCS 8. At the back of the hospital. If you open up a back door, you'll run into us," she said, wincing at her own word choice.

"No problem. I'll take care of you," I told the guy, even though I doubted he understood much. Under the blood and swollen eyes, he looked white, maybe age 30, slight build, 5'7", with a little blondish moustache painted in blood. "What's your name?"

Of course he didn't answer me.

"What do you think he's doing back here?" Tori murmured to me. No one used the back doors except people who worked here, and even then, it was usually easier to take one of the major doors. "Does he look familiar to you?"

I shook my head. I'm no good at recognizing people who've been bashed up, but I would have remembered a guy who was more my size. "Are they sending an ambulance?"

Tori smiled briefly. "They're sending a stretcher. I called emerg."

Brilliant move. Central 911 might get bogged down in designating which team to dispatch, but the man lay only steps away from an emergency room.

Granted, not a trauma ER, but this guy needed stabilization and CT even faster than Mireille.

"What are the chances of two head traumas in one morning?" I muttered to myself. "In and around our parking lot?"

Tori turned to me, her lips parting, her eyes wide. And somehow, I knew that she'd had a vision of a ghost.

23

HOPE

A second later, I could *feel* the ghost myself.

The air thickened, almost like the molecules had expanded and grown gelatinous, although still transparent enough for me to make out Tori's dilated pupils. Her lips moved. She spoke to the ghost, and I strained to listen.

I picked up a low, indistinct hum, the way I imagined elephants speak. Vibrations moved through the soles of my feet and, strangely, into my nipples and the nape of my neck.

I clenched my fists, cutting my palms with my own nails, and tried to breathe. That meant inhaling that weird air, but so what. I needed to survive the next few minutes, even if ghost fog gave me cancer in five years.

Tori shouted now over the roaring in my ears. I couldn't make out any words, but her neck tendons strained and the whites showed around her eyes.

I closed my eyes to hear better, and the ghost fog choked me. Like trying to breathe in soup. Or getting waterboarded. I clawed at the air, internally screaming.

The ghost disappeared.

My head whirled. I could breathe again, but my feet didn't know it. I thumped down on the pavement, butt first.

"Hope! Get up, Hope!"

Tori's fingers tore at my shirt. I knew I should obey her, but I couldn't. "Sorry," I mouthed.

"They're coming! Get up!"

Who? I tried to focus and realized, whoops, two paramedics, Cathleen, and other ER folk bore down on us with a stretcher, wheels rattling on the pavement, while I sank down beside the bleeding patient.

Wait, wait. I could do this. I found my hands and pressed the pavement. Rocks under my palms. Ow. Nope.

Tori yanked under my armpits while I pushed myself up again. I managed to get my knees under me without stepping on Tori's feet and swayed up to standing, Tori still propping me upright.

"What's going on?" Cathleen spared me a withering glance while a female paramedic attached a C-spine collar to the man and another lowered the stretcher to the ground.

Tori explained how we found the man as a third person affixed a face mask to give the man oxygen.

"Aren't you the same resident who found Dr. Laroque this morning?" Cathleen asked Tori.

Tori kept her cool. "Yes. I hope I don't find a third person today."

"Jamais deux sans trois," said Cathleen, with a heavy accent, but we all understood that bad things come in threes. Hard to imagine anything worse than Dr. Burns and two hit and runs in our own parking lot. I'd already scored three bad things. Four, if you counted the ghost.

I took another breath of clean, ghost-free air and made my way to the paramedics. "Need any help?"

The shortest paramedic shook her head. "You take care of yourself," she said, not unkindly. Even though I felt 200 percent better, I must've looked wobbly.

"What's up with the princess and the pea over there?" Cathleen asked Tori. "She can't handle blood?"

I glowered when I realized she meant me, but Tori replied coolly, "Hope's seen more blood than a vampire. I gave her bad news right before you came. If you'll excuse us, I have clinic."

"If you say so." Cathleen raised dubious eyebrows at me before she followed the paramedics back to the ER. I started to follow them, but Tori drew me aside first.

"Do not engage," said Tori.

She meant Cathleen. I grinned self-consciously. "Was I so obvious?"

"You may not say it, but your face is shouting. You okay?"

I shivered. Cathleen and company had wheeled out of earshot already, if we kept our voices down. I fixed my eyes on the blood-spattered pavement and said, "I felt the ghost."

"I could tell. Walk with me to clinic."

I fell in step with her. I had no idea where we were going, but it didn't matter. "What did the ghost say?"

Her smile vanished. "It was more visual. Someone on a motorcycle."

"The ghost was on a *motorcycle?*" That blew my mind. I pictured pale ghost maidens roaming the moors and wringing their hands, not gunning for the highway.

"Yeah. Going fast around a corner."

"That sounds bad."

"But even before rounding the corner, the tire hit something else. At least that's what it felt like, because I lost control of the bike and flew through the air."

"Hold up!" I gazed around the parking lot. "You were *inside* the ghost?"

"Yes. It doesn't happen often, but this time ... " She shrugged.

"Okay, wild. You think the ghost was our guy in the parking lot"—now on a gurney trundling toward the ER—"trying to communicate what happened to him?"

Tori shook her head. "He's not dead. So he's not a ghost."

I had to grin at her logic. "Fair."

"And the curve wasn't anywhere around here?" I gestured at the parking lot.

Tori shook her head. "It didn't look like here. He was in the mountains, and it was fall. The leaves were turning."

Interesting. Although Montreal is hilly, the neighbouring Ottawa Valley is quite flat because during the last ice age, passing glaciers took out all the mountains. You have to travel to the Laurentians or upstate New York for skiing.

So the ghost hadn't shown itself to Tori at St. Joe's in May. But why had it sprung that vision on Tori, and a little on me?

"Were you knocked out too?" I asked. "That was intense."

Tori shook her head. "I'm used to it."

I felt like a wuss, but tried to shake that off. First ghost of your life's gotta traumatize you somehow. "What about Griffin?" Her boyfriend might have experienced one of Tori's ghosts too.

She smiled. "Griffin has a thick skin."

Huh.

"Don't feel bad. Most people can't detect a ghost at all. You can, a little. It's a talent, right?"

"I guess." Honestly, if I had a choice, I'd rather either stay impervious and indifferent, or enable full ghost ESP like Tori. Right now, it felt like the worst of both worlds. I could only sense enough to get knocked off my feet.

BEEP BEEP BEEP BEEP BEEP

I silenced my pager and read the little screen.

CODE TRAUMA

ER

24

NOVEMBER 10, 14:54

GORDON

Aside from the newspaper article, Gordon found no other concrete trace of Nadia Smith. With 27,000,000 hits on Google today, let alone decades ago, he couldn't pin her down.

Smith was the most common last name in Saskatchewan.

Even more strangely, although Vlad Vrac had graduated from high school (hard to find records going back that far, but Vlad had been the valedictorian), Gordon found no evidence that Mikhail had graduated.

Had he dropped out, or had something happened to Mikhail?

25

MAY 22, 12:55

HOPE

I hurried to the resuscitation bay. Our man from the parking lot now laid on a stretcher in the C-spine collar, hooked up to the monitor and surrounded by personnel. His right hand still twitched, but he'd stopped groaning, which meant the bleeding in his brain had probably expanded.

Bad. Very bad.

Dr. Chia stood at the foot of the bed, in the trauma team leader position, where she could view the monitors.

"Got an 18 gauge," muttered the nurse inserting an IV in the left antecubital fossa, the fold in the elbow. They always say to use 16 gauge and bigger in a trauma, but this wasn't a trauma hospital. Maybe we didn't have 16 gauges.

"Great." Singh faced me from the head of the bed, the respiratory therapist and airway equipment at his side. He'd claimed the airway position and now named his medications. "I need 20 of Etomidate and 150 of Sux."

Cheng applied the ultrasound machine to the man's right chest, checking for a pneumothorax (dangerous air in the chest, aka pneumo) or hemothorax (bleeding in the chest, aka hemo).

"I'll put in a line," I said aloud, but the nurses installed two more IVs, rendering me useless.

"You're the one who found him?" Dr. Chia asked me.

"Dr. Yamamoto and I found him unconscious in the parking lot. She called for help immediately." I glanced at the C-spine collar and prayed that I hadn't shifted his neck while the ghost possessed Tori's body.

"Someone must've hit him," Cheng muttered, lifting the ultrasound probe. "He has a pneumo. I'm on it. Give me the biggest chest tube you've got." He turned to me. "What size gloves are you?"

"Six." Yay, Cheng! Surgery types can turn possessive about procedures. He could have cut me out and claimed, *You're just family medicine, you don't need to know this.* But I hungered for experience after my single chest tube in medical school.

"Did you see any car leaving the parking lot?" Singh asked from the top of the bed as he prepared to intubate with video laryngoscopy.

I shook my head. "We'd come from Peloquin." That meant the front of the main hospital. The car should've passed us before it left.

"Unless they exited out the back, to Jean Brillant," the RT muttered, ready to hook the Ambu bag to the endotracheal tube.

No matter which exit, the car had vanished by the time Tori and I had come around.

"Want to do the 16 gauge needle?" asked Cheng.

"You are a prince among men." I accepted the needle and began landmarking. Mid clavicular (collar bone) line, second intercostal (rib) space. The collar bone jutted out because the guy was skinny.

A patient with a pneumothorax, or a hole in the lung, can develop a tension pneumo. That's the most dangerous kind because the air around the lung keeps expanding within the chest cavity, preventing the lung itself from inflating.

Or you can have an open pneumo, where the hole in the chest wall communicates with the outside air. Either way, the treatment is the same: jab a hole in the chest wall and let the bad air out through the tube.

I plunged my angiocather (needle and sheath combo) into the spot, then removed the needle. Air whizzed out through the plastic sheath, confirming the diagnosis.

I beamed behind my mask. I'd never done a needle decompression. For my first chest tube, a non-trauma, we'd seen the pneumo on X-ray and I'd moved straight to chest tube. But in this case, we needed immediate decompression before definitive management with a chest tube.

Cheng nodded in approval as I prepped the chest tube area with the Chlorhexidine he'd poured in the tray, smearing a sponge over the patient's skin. Once, twice, three times.

"Good. Exactly. And go above the rib," said Cheng.

"Yes, to avoid the neurovascular bundle." We want to avoid the artery, vein, and nerve running beneath each rib.

He smiled at me. "Good woman. Yep, fourth intercostal space, I like it."

I swiftly landmarked the rib with my fingers, cut the skin above the bone with a scalpel, separated the muscles with a Kelly forceps, advanced with my fingers—

A terribly familiar voice sliced through the emergency department. "You're only supposed to call me directly if it's life or death!" Vrac hollered. *"Is this life or death?"*

26

DECEMBER 15, 08:15

GORDON

"I have a brother," Gordon volunteered loudly one day in the OR. He had to speak up. He'd been assigned to both Dr. Vrac and Dr. Burns, probably because of pre-Christmas shortages. This chance would never come again.

Dr. Burns frowned at him, but Vrac overheard and said, "Yeah? Who cares?"

Gordon figured his heart banged hard enough that you could take his pulse from across the room, but he answered anyway. "I'm doing a research paper on brothers, the similarities and differences between them."

"How is that related to—" Dr. Burns started to say.

"I get it!" Vrac interrupted. "Anesthesia is so boring that you gotta write papers about genetics! Okay then, what do you want to know?"

Gordon ignored the usual slight on his profession. "I'm also gathering anecdotal data before I do genetic testing. I want to know if phenotypical and genotypical similarities correspond with anecdotal history."

Dr. Burns shook his head, but Dr. Vrac said cheerfully, "A buncha gobbledygook for you eggheads. All right, I'm game. What do you want to know?"

"Do you have a brother?" Gordon asked.

Dr. Vrac shook his head. "I'm not playing that game."

"I could give you a survey, and if you wanted to give a DNA sample, and then pass a DNA kit onto your brother—"

"Shut the fuck up," said Vrac, turning back to the case. "Anyone else say anything about brothers in this OR, I'll cut your fuckin' nuts off."

Boom. Gordon knew that he was on the right track, but how could he gather any more data when he'd run out of town records, and Dr. Vrac refused to utter another word?

27

MAY 22, 13:08

HOPE

Vrac startled me so badly that my fingers jerked.

"Careful with the sharps!" Dr. Chia called. She touched her abdomen briefly under her white coat. I wondered if she was pregnant before I let the thought go. You can't get distracted during a trauma.

"Let me?" Cheng asked.

I stepped back to let him in, and Cheng took over with his sterile gloves while Dr. Chia gathered her composure and said, "Airway secured. End tidal CO_2 38. Breathing—pneumothorax decompressed, preparing for chest tube." Singh had successfully tubed to make sure air could get to the lungs, and Cheng and I would get the lungs working properly.

Dr. Vrac ripped open the curtain that's supposed to shield the patient. He strode toward us without bothering to close it behind him. "Why didn't you take him to UC?"

"Closest hospital, Dr. Vrac," said a paramedic. So even the medics knew him.

"I don't give a fuck if this is the closest hospital. St. Joe's not a trauma hospital, you stupid piece of—"

Dr. Chia raised her voice to recap and bring people's attention back to the case. "Blood pressure 89/45, pulse 110, sat 92 percent, left pupil blown, GCS 7 before sedation—"

Shock, most likely hemorrhagic (bleeding too much), lungs borderline for a young person, brain impaired ...

"Thank you, Captain Obvious!" Vrac yelled, coming over to stare directly at the patient's face.

I sucked in my breath. Bad enough that he talked to me like this. But a full ER physician and a paramedic? In front of the entire team?

Vrac snapped his head back up and glared at us like we were the ones who'd run the man over. "You need to ship him out of here. Stat."

"We're stabilizing the patient," Dr. Chia replied.

"You hear what I said?" Vrac crossed the room so he could shout in her face, almost nose to nose. "Transfer, transfer, transfer!"

"Stabilize, then transfer." Her calm voice cut through his bluster.

"Leave it to the experts. You're just a family doctor with what, one extra year of training?"

Dr. Chia's cheeks flushed, but she clung to her temper. "Family doctors are the backbone of the health care system."

I nodded in firm agreement. Every study shows that family doctors save the health care system money by preventing problems like diabetic complications and minimizing unnecessary testing. Anyone who trivializes family physicians has, at best, a microscopic penis and even less common sense.

Vrac glared at me. "What are you looking at? What are you doing here, Sneeze?"

My turn to redden. I hated that nickname, and the fact that now everyone in the ER would call me Sneeze.

"Anyone who rolls through these doors is my patient," said Dr. Chia. "Dr. Sze is welcome. If you don't want to be involved in his care, that's your decision."

"Are you kicking me out? You don't want the general surgery team here?" Vrac grinned, his teeth gleaming under the fluorescent lights. He hadn't bothered to slap on a face mask or gloves. "How's the ER going to handle it when my team has one hand in the chest and the other in the airway? If that's the way you want it, that's how you're gonna get it. No problem. We outta here!"

28

DECEMBER 16, 10:00

GORDON

Gordon called the high school with low hopes. Since Dr. Vrac was 62, his teachers would be 85 and up, long retired and perhaps dead.

"Meadowvale High School," said a pleasant older woman.

"Hi, I'm from A1 Marketing," Gordon said. "I'm reaching out to the schools of our alumni to see if you could predict your high achievers before they hit university!"

"Excuse me?" the woman said.

"I'm conducting a research survey regarding previous graduates."

"Hold the line, please. I'll transfer you to the principal, Ms. Cortese."

"Thanks." He waited for the principal and repeated his spiel.

"Where are you calling from?" a woman's low voice replied.

"We're A1, a private institution conducting a survey ... "

"Hang on. I'll look you up," she said, making his heart rate double. After a pause, the principal added, "You're based in Colorado?"

"Yes, but we're expanding our research base, and Meadowvale could be a part of it!"

"What are you selling." Her voice creaked like she was either in her 60s or a smoker.

"Not selling a single thing," said Gordon, although he could've made a

fortune vending his own sweat at this rate. "I'm conducting interviews with successful previous graduates from your school and their teachers."

"You must be thinking of someone in particular."

"Yes, we'll start with Dr. Vladimir Vrac. He's now a surgeon at McGill University!"

The principal paused so long that Gordon thought she'd hung up. Finally, she spoke. "You won't find anyone else here who remembers Waldo."

"Waldo," he repeated.

"He didn't like his name. His nickname was Vlado, so he asked us to call him Waldo. Not that it helped."

"Fascinating. He prefers Vadim now."

"That sounds familiar. I wonder if his brother called him that."

Gordon struggled not to stutter. "You kn-knew his brother too?"

She paused. "I don't believe this will help with your article. You probably want a feel-good piece."

"Investigative journalism."

"Ah. Still, you probably have a dozen different sources—"

"You're my best one so far. Could I take you out to coffee? Please?"

"I'm a busy woman, and you're calling from a Montreal area code."

"I'll make it an espresso and a virtual coffee if you like."

"You're a funny man." She cleared her throat. "As it happens, I'm coming to your city for the holidays. Let's see if we can work something out."

29

MAY 22, 13:11

HOPE

Vrac waved us out the door while the nurses murmured in protest and Dr. Chia said, "You can't do this!"

"Yeah? Watch me. Come on, boys!"

Singh slowly stepped away from the airway and the RT took his place.

"Cheng! You hear me?"

"Just a minute!" I said brightly, as if Dr. Vrac were banging on a toilet stall door instead of dragging us away from patient care. My pal Cheng continued to install the chest tube.

"Get going, Sneeze," said Vrac. "Now."

"Okay!" I slowly removed my gloves, trying to draw Vrac's eyes away from Cheng. *Come on, come on.* Dr. Chia or Sébastien, the second year family medicine resident, could take over the chest tube, but ideally, Dr. Chia would run the code without the distraction of procedures, and Cheng could do this faster than me or Sébastien.

"Don't punish the patient with your anger," Dr. Chia said, and Vrac began to blister her with his tongue.

Pop.

The air gushed out of the patient's chest hard enough to blow my bangs up. Cheng's whole body stiffened as he passed the chest tube.

Roxanne had already connected the tube to the drain. We all watched the air bubbles undulate before blood gushed out.

"I hope the tube's big enough," Cheng muttered, before he said to me, "Sorry, Sze. Next one's yours." Cheng reached for the suture material while Vrac screamed at us, "Move out, move out, what the hell is wrong with you?"

Sébastien slid between us and the patient to stabilize the tube, and Roxanne passed him the suture material instead.

"You good sewing this in?" Cheng asked him.

"Not only can I sew it in, I could have put it in," replied Sébastien. Oops. We'd stepped on a few toes by blasting into the ER and grabbing the best procedures."Sorry," I said before we got carted away.

"Can't believe my fucking eyes," Vrac fumed as we hurried out of the resuscitation bay. "This never happened when I was a resident. You obviously never want to operate, Cheng. You can't hear a basic order."

"So sorry, sir," said Cheng. "In the middle of a procedure, I zone out. It won't happen again."

"Of course it won't. This isn't a trauma hospital. This is a *bumfuck nowhere* hospital."

An elderly patient on a hallway gurney who was waiting for a bed upstairs raised his eyebrows at Dr. Vrac, but the surgeon didn't bother lowering his voice as he led us past the old light boxes and out the exit.

"It was only my second chest tube," I piped up. "I'm sorry if I distracted—"

Suddenly, I had Vrac's full attention. He peered directly into my face. "Your second chest tube. What kind of bullshit is that? What year resident are you?"

"First year."

"At the end of your first year, right?"

"Getting there."

"And you've only done one-and-a-half chest tubes?" He gave a scornful cackle, the way he might laugh at a 50-year-old man who'd confessed he was a virgin.

It would have been two if you hadn't stopped me. I opened my mouth to say so, but one look from Singh stopped me.

"You're supposed to graduate in just over a year! What kind of shit are medical schools pumping out now?"

"Hard to imagine when there are such spectacular examples of what they used to pump out," I replied. Singh's eyes widened, and Cheng shook his head, but Vrac didn't seem to notice.

He pounded his chest and called out to the sky. "What'd I do to deserve this? How'd I get stuck with this bunch of dumb, coloured fucks?"

30

MAY 22, 13:25

HOPE

"Everything's fuckin' going downhill!" Vrac yelled. The patients in the hallway, and their caregivers, tried to draw back from him, while he ranted on. "How many times did I have to repeat my fucking self? Everyone's an idiot except me. I need to do a fuckin' IQ test before we let anyone else into the country and, better yet, onto my service."

I truly needed to say something. The only thing nailing my mouth shut was the fact that Vrac could fail me on this rotation, which would torpedo my application to the emergency program when I graduated from family medicine.

You got the death OR, I heard the medical student say again.

I sure did. First someone technically killed Dr. Burns. Then my attending made me walk away from a trauma case to prove he had a bigger dick than the female emergency physician. My self-respect eroded with every word I had to endure, and it wasn't even 2 p.m.

"That woman should stick to having babies and leave medicine to the real men," Vrac raged on. "Imagine if I had to repeat myself ten times in the OR. That would be dangerous. We need to have one leader. One. Leader."

I traipsed up the stairs after him. *Yes, that's the whole point of trauma team leaders.* DR. CHIA WAS THE LEADER.

"Guess we'll see how Dr. Chia does without us," said Cheng.

"Exactly! See how that twat likes it when I pull away everyone who's actually doing something! You see that fruity resident, totally pissed that you did the chest tube? If he wanted it, he should have gone for it. That's what we did in my day!"

We should play a drinking game where we took a shot at every insult. Racist, sexist, homophobic ...

"Now get back to the floor while I scare up some more business. Some of those gas docs owe me one, you know what I'm saying?"

Yes. You will bully anesthesia into doing whatever you want to do. Or kill them outright, like Dr. Burns.

Except Cheng gave Vrac an alibi, and Vrac had lost money not operating today. Yet if Vrac hadn't stabbed Dr. Burns, who had?

Vrac picked up the pace and bumped into a plastic garbage can in the hallway. Without breaking his stride, he scooped the can and tossed it across the lobby, where it rolled before the lid burst off.

Garbage spilled out on the ground, mostly takeout containers and old coffee cups, but also napkins, gloves, and sadly, a worn-out colouring book.

"They should clean up around here!" Vrac shouted over his shoulder.

I glanced at the guys to check if he meant us. Singh gave a tiny shake of his head, so we followed Vrac with trash in our wake. Appropriate.

"Serves them right. Everything here is garbage. It sure wasn't like this when I was a resident. You won't catch them shoving garbage cans in your way at UC!"

No one was safe from a Vrac attack. Not surgical residents, not emergency doctors, not men, not women. Not even trash cans.

I tried not to picture an elderly woman slipping on greasy cardboard, or a child diving for the leftover fries.

Dr. Vladimir "Vance" Vrac posed a menace to society, quite possibly to the point of death. Now I had to prove it.

31

DECEMBER 20, 11:30

GORDON

Gordon met the principal, Ms. Cortese, on a park bench outside a grocery store. He tried to ignore the crunch of crusty snow breaking under his buttocks. "Hello, I'm Gordon. Nice to meet you. Are you sure you don't want to go to a café? My treat."

Ms. Cortese shook her head. "Let's get this over with. Part of the reason I'm talking to you ... it was a different time." She pulled a cigarette package out of her purse. "You don't mind?"

As an anesthesia resident, Gordon hated smoking. Now he knew why she'd insisted on meeting outside, despite both their breaths coalescing in the cold air. He hid a grimace. "Go ahead."

She fumbled with her lighter. He held his hand out, offering to help. Then he lit her cigarette for her, enabling her behaviour, but she'd smoke either way.

She blew smoke at his face in gratitude. "That's better."

He forced a smile.

"Ah, you don't smoke. Well, you'll live longer." She blew her next puff away from him. "I was a resource teacher then, barely graduated from teacher's college. I was only there for a month before I moved to Calgary with my boyfriend, but I remember Waldo and Mike."

He tried not to blink at the anglicization of both their names.

"They tried to fit in, but kids can tell when something's off. Even if their clothes were okay, sometimes neater and cleaner than the other kids, they gave off this feeling of ... " She smoked some more. "For Waldo, it was this desperate energy to be the best. Best student, best at soccer—he wasn't the most talented player, but by God, he played dirty. If he got a red card, he'd smile and scream in victory when his team scored. He scared the others. They wouldn't hang around him."

The man hadn't changed much.

"Don't put that in your article," she added. "Are you recording this?"

Should he? "Only if you want me to," he said.

She shook her head. "Everything's off the record. I shouldn't talk to you, but I'm so old, no one cares anymore."

Gordon did a brief calculation. If she'd been, say, 23 when Vrac was 16, she'd be 69 now. Not elderly, but certainly old enough to retire on a teacher's pension, or whatever principals made.

"Mike, well, he worshipped Waldo. He joined soccer, he worked hard at school. Whatever his big brother did, he did too. But he was like a carbon copy. Not as tall, not as strong, not as bright. He tried hard, though. And he was nicer. The kids liked him better. He had friends." She tapped the ash from her cigarette.

Gordon swivelled his legs away from the ashes. "That might be a fair trade off."

She shook her head. "They loved each other, but they both wanted what the other one had. Waldo wanted people to like him, not only fear him. Mike wanted to be the best. But they were always there for each other."

Gordon raised his eyebrows questioningly.

She showed her teeth. "You don't miss much. I knew it was because the mother wasn't there for them. By high school, a lot of parents have backed off. Or they had back then, anyway, it's different now with helicopter parents in your face all the time, how's my boy doing, how dare you give him a D, she's the smartest girl in the school, her grandmother just died. And others ... "

"Not tiger moms?" Gordon asked.

She snorted, almost dropping her cigarette. "That was before the term was invented. However, suffice to say, they were not tiger parents, no."

Gordon struggled to keep the conversation going. "You think the parents beat them?"

She shook her head. "I never had any proof. I had a bad feeling. I even asked the soccer coach to keep an eye on Waldo in the change room. He never saw a mark."

"So ... "

"So either they were clever enough not to hit him where anyone could see easily, or it was the opposite. They ignored the two boys. Which leaves its own kind of mark, and is very hard to prove." She sucked deeply on the cigarette, exaggerating the lines around her mouth. "I couldn't document anything to report to Children's Aid. They weren't underweight, they did their homework, they had extracurricular activities, and like I said, they dressed well. But the parents never once came for parent-teacher interviews, never showed up for a game. I asked Waldo what they did for a living, and he said, 'This and that.'"

Gordon frowned. "Do you think they were drug addicts?"

"I thought maybe alcoholics. I called home once when Mike was late with an assignment. No one answered the phone. I left a message, and the next day, Waldo came to see me, red-faced, telling me that he would act as Mike's guardian and I should never call home again. I should come see him if anything went wrong. That wasn't on the official school papers, so I tried calling again. Still no answer. I drove by their apartment once or twice."

More than twice, Gordon figured, but he kept his mouth shut.

"I never saw a parent." She finished the cigarette, dropped it on the pavement, and ground the butt with the toe of her shoe. "So I never proved anything was wrong at that home."

Gordon nodded.

"If you write anything I said, I'll deny it."

"Then why did you talk to me?" Gordon blurted out. She obviously hadn't stayed in Alberta with that boyfriend. She'd returned to Saskatchewan and become a principal at the same school where she'd taught as a new grad.

"Curiosity." She flashed a grin at him, and he glimpsed the younger woman lurking inside her. "They always puzzled me, and I never solved the puzzle."

Gordon knew that if ever he did write a piece, Vrac could easily identify her. How many of his former teachers would still work in schools today?

She answered the question before he asked. "I know you won't write any article about this, Gordon. I know you don't belong to any institute. If you do write anything, I'll come right after you."

He chose not to speak instead of stuttering a reply. She winked at him before she lit another cigarette, and he mulled over her words. Was it possible the mother had abandoned Waldo and Mike? That no parents existed at all?

32

MAY 22, 13:40

HOPE

"Now fuck off and do something useful!" Vrac hollered.

Cheng waited until Vrac and Singh had disappeared down the fluorescent hall stuffed with patients, then said, "Go eat."

"I'm not hungry."

"Then lie down before the shit hits the fan. I'll handle the floor until then."

Cheng wanted to protect me. I smiled at him and headed to the second floor residents' lounge to grab my water bottle.

"Hey, Hope."

I spun around the hallway to face Tucker, my ex-fiancé and still one of the two most magnificent loves of my life. He stood by the elevator with Mireille's savaged bike, her bright blue helmet drooping off one handlebar.

Tucker had shaved his white hair to near-skull level after we broke up, which startled me every time I saw him. His skull looked naked to me.

"Hi." I turned bright red. My glasses slipped down my nose, and I sensed the sweat in my hair. Not cool. "Uh, you picked up Mireille's bike?" I asked, even though no one else's bike had acquired scoliosis.

He rolled his eyes. "She was so set on it that I got the keys from Tori. I know it's not repairable."

Irreparable like our relationship. I silently followed him into the elevator, a Pied Piper with a broken bike instead of a flute. The doors banged shut behind us.

Avoiding Tucker's eyes, I examined where the bike's blue paint had been rubbed down to metal on the bike's left side. Then I jabbed my finger at a smear of white paint on the naked steel. "Wait. Are you seeing what I'm seeing?"

Tucker bent his shorn head down to examine it before he nodded, face grim.

I brought up a picture of Mireille's bike model on my phone and showed it to him. "That's not part of the original paint job. She didn't fall off her bike. I bet someone hit her with a white car."

The elevator pinged to a stop on the fourth floor. The doors opened, but neither of us moved. Then I stabbed the button for the sixth floor. "Let's move the bike somewhere safe, like my call room, to keep it as evidence. Can you call the police?"

Tucker hesitated. "I'm on call, but sure." The elevator door pinged open, and he coaxed the bike forward. "We shouldn't have moved her bike."

"You're right, but we didn't know that." The elevator tried to close on us while I looked for the upside. "Paint is still forensic evidence."

"I know, but they should've set up markers on the scene, looking for blood and hair and tire marks."

Mireille's bloody curls flashed through my mind. I spoke to distract myself. "Too late. Cars have completely destroyed the scene by now. Police can use this paint to figure it out. When a vehicle hit her, paint got transferred to her bike, along with kinetic energy." I gestured at the caved-in frame. Pedestrians and cyclists get killed fairly often in Montreal. Aggressive drivers, fearless cyclists, few bike lanes, steep hills, bad weather, and potholed pavement make a lethal combination. I pointed down the hall to the right, toward my call room.

Tucker shook his head and closed his eyes. "She's lucky to be alive."

I nodded and touched his arm without thinking. His triceps tensed under my fingers, and I cleared my throat. "Sorry."

Tucker took a step away and paved over the awkward moment. "The paint transfer doesn't prove anything. Mireille could have hit a white car when she went flying."

"Like you said, the police can use special units to recreate the scene if they want." I wished I knew more about car accidents or physics or trajectory. If only I could ask my other ex, Ryan Wu, the engineer.

"I've biked with Mireille," Tucker said, maneuvering the bike. "She cuts through traffic, but she installed extra mirrors on her bike and even on her helmet." He whistled a few notes.

I stopped pulling the key out of my scrubs. "Isn't that the song 'Young Men Dead'?"

"Oh, yeah, I heard you were asking about it and it got stuck in my head. You know they used that song in the show 'True Detective'?"

"No." And who cared. Only a month ago, Tucker and I would've snuck into my call room to say howdy.

"Here, I'll show you." He brought up the video on his phone. The first dark notes sounded through the room. "Oops, right song, but that's a BMW X1 commercial. Here's the right one."

I ground my teeth. Instead of tearing off my clothes, Tucker showed me fucking YouTube commercials! When the steam stopped pouring out of my nostrils, I said, "I'll talk to Kevin." My nine-year-old brother handles computers like an extension of his brain. "And wait a minute. Mireille had a camera on her helmet!"

"Looks pretty smashed," said Tucker, checking it. "I don't want to take out the microSD card. I'll leave it for the cops."

"Still. They should get something from it. We can actually see what happened."

He nodded. "If the card still works."

Damn. A pager beeped beeped beeped beeped. We checked our waist bands to see who was the lucky winner.

Tucker lifted his black pager in the air. "Later. I'll call the police when I have a chance. But do you really want them going in your call room?"

I made a face. I guard my sleep like rubies.

"Let's move it to my room. It makes more sense since I'm calling them."

"Thanks. Are you sure you're okay with that, especially when we've moved the evidence?"

"Positive. And I don't have to deal with The Impaler." Tucker grinned at me, making my heart flip over. I still loved him, whatever good it did me. Unrequited love feels only slightly better than *I fell in l love with two guys at once and neither one will never forgive me.*

I texted a few quick photos to Kevin before Tucker ported the bike away, already answering the page through speakerphone since he needed both hands to maneuver.

Gotta love that brain.

And shoulders. And bum. And legs. And, well, everything.

Something Tori had said rang in my memory. *He's so good at pretending his heart isn't broken. Almost as good as you.*

Tori. I needed to tell her about Mireille vs. the white car. I yearned to ask her about the ghost. And I absolutely had to distract myself from Tucker's rear end.

I locked the door and pulled out my phone right as my own pager rang, dragging me back to the ER.

33

DECEMBER 21, 08:51

GORDON

Principal Cortese had dropped an old yearbook on the bench between herself and Gordon. "Keep it," she'd said, coughing into her palm. "I've got too much of that old crap."

Gordon had examined the young faces of "Waldo" and "Mike" Vrac and launched an investigation made easier with their nicknames but hampered by the holidays. Worse, child protection services had sealed any records. No former teachers would talk to him.

Principal Cortese laughed when he called her again. "Half of them are dead, or lost their marbles, or don't want to remember some poor kid from 40 years ago. Good luck."

"You don't have any leads?" Gordon asked, hating the begging tone in his own voice.

She snorted. "Leads from four decades ago?"

"I can't figure out what happened to their mother or even Mike."

"You know what you need? A private investigator in Regina who can cut through the red tape and find the documents for you."

That made a lot of sense. "Do you have any recommendations?"

"Sure. Jimmy Stanton. I'll send you his contact information."

"A friend of yours?" Gordon asked.

Principal Cortese chuckled. "Everyone's a friend in Regina. You want his information or not?"

Gordon sighed. "Send it."

34

MAY 22, 14:29

HOPE

The smell of poop hit me as soon as I flung open the side ER door.

I paused, eyes watering. Two of the stretcher patients' heads swivelled toward me. Bed alarms screeched in my ears.

Roxanne waved her good arm at me. "Hey, stranger."

"You doing a double?" I checked my watch. Heading into evening shift for her now.

She mimed swiping dollar bills off her stump.

I laughed. "What's up? For general surgery," I added, because even though Roxanne has a great memory, no harm reminding her when she's doing a double.

"You need to take another look at the trauma. He's going south."

I took a deep breath. "Dr. Vrac knows I'm reassessing him?"

"Let's just say that Dr. Chia chose to page the residents first, starting with you." She grinned at me even as worry creased her brown eyes.

"He's crashing?"

"Yup. We stabilized him, but he really needs to go out. We're not a trauma hospital. No one has any beds, so in the meantime, general surgery's the closest we got."

"Ouch." A non-trauma general surgery team at a non-trauma hospital with no willing surgeon. I made my way to the resus room and stared at the man in the bed.

The first thing that struck me was the greyish cast to the patient's skin. His chest tube bubbled with every breath. His numbers weren't so bad—108/70, 108, 92%, 18, end tidal CO2 of 36—but he looked terrible.

"His CT shows a grade III splenic laceration."

"Hmm." It sure sounded operative to me. The question was if Dr. Vrac would agree to open this poor guy up, or if he'd let him die to prove the point that St. Joe's wasn't a trauma hospital and that the ER doc couldn't manage without him.

I called Cheng before I finished typing up my consult. I read the CT report to him verbatim and concluded, "We're going to have to sell this to Vrac."

"How?" He sounded like he was chewing.

"I don't know. But I don't want to lose this guy. You have any ideas?"

"A pretty nurse always cheers him up."

I snorted.

"I'm serious. Who's his nurse?"

"Roxanne told me about him. You know, big brown eyes, one arm?"

"Yeah, he likes Roxanne. I remember him making a joke about how the one arm is good because she'd work harder to please him."

I choked before I managed to get out, "I don't think—"

"Okay, I'll try to sell it to him. Is Dr. Chia around?"

Dr. Chia watched me from the doorway, her lovely face drawn with tension.

"Yup. At the bedside."

"If you can keep her away from him, that would help."

"I have another consult for you in 5," Dr. Chia told me.

I covered the phone, even though Cheng might want to know anyway. "Another one?"

"The fun never stops. She's a 56-year-old female."

Uh oh on a few levels. General surgeons often complain that they can't tell if the abdominal pain is from an appendix or the female genital tract. They kick cases to obstetrics and gynecology ("Can't rule out ovarian pathology"), and Ob/gyn punts back ("This is clearly a bowel problem"), leaving the patient stuck in no-woman's-land.

You'd think that ultrasounds or CTs would rule everything out, but they don't. CTs give a much sharper picture, along with a side order of radiation, but they're easily messed up if the patient moves too much, and they don't show some organs like the liver, gall bladder, uterus, or ovaries as well as ultrasounds.

The ultrasound's sound waves get blocked by gas, food, or a less skilled technician, but don't subject you to radiation. Because they're hands-on, we lose access to ultrasounds after hours. I checked my watch. Still before 4 p.m. We might make it.

MRI's are good for soft tissue, but you usually have to wait months for those. Not on the menu.

So sometimes the patient needs two different scans, and even then, we don't have the answer by the time I see them in the ER.

I glanced at the new chart and drew back the curtain on bed 5. A stocky woman with short grey hair, no makeup, in sport socks along with the usual surgical gown, stared at me above her puke bag before she raised a few fingers in greeting.

Uh oh again. She looked low maintenance. The opposite of those who show up every 24 hours, demanding a million dollar workup for their "incredible pain." You find nothing wrong, they curse you, and they return in 24 hours.

But low maintenance people only come in if they're fixing to die.

"Hello, Madame," I said. "I'm Dr. Hope Sze, resident doctor on general surgery. Our service has been asked to see you. I understand that you've had abdominal pain for a week. Could you show me where?"

She gestured at her entire belly and even her chest.

"Can you point with one finger?" We want to localize the pain.

She shook her head, thought about it, and pressed both hands to her belly before she flinched and heaved a bit of spit into her bag. She still hadn't said a word.

I glanced at her vital signs. 149/90, 91, 92%, 22. Like the other A case, the numbers looked better than the patient.

"How bad is your pain on 10? Ten is like someone ripping your leg off."

She thought about it and held up nine fingers. She'd already gotten morphine half an hour ago.

"And you've been having nausea and vomiting? How often are you vomiting?"

She held up 10 fingers.

"Ten times today? Do you take marijuana?" Every ER shift, I explain cannabis hyperemesis syndrome. Yes, marijuana can make you puke non-stop. Yes, even if you smoked it for years. Yes, even if you don't smoke much. Hot showers give temporary relief, but you have to give up weed completely for three to six months to really get it out of your system.

She nodded to the ten times today and shook her head for marijuana. Hooray.

"Okay. Is the vomiting getting better, worse, or the same?"

She made a face.

"Worse. Okay, thank you. Let me go through your surgical history. Laparoscopic hiatal hernia repair three years ago?"

Nod.

"Tubal ligation 20 years ago?"

Nod. She closed her eyes as if even that had exhausted her.

"Thank you." I ran through her medications for blood pressure, cholesterol, and depression—pretty standard stuff—and tried to smile at her while I did a quick exam. No bowel sounds, and she moaned softly when I touched her belly, especially the left upper quadrant (LUQ).

I quickly stepped away and applied hand sanitizer as I said, "Your imaging shows that you probably have a gastric volvulus, which is when your stomach twists around itself 180 degrees." We talk about volvulus for children, but I'd never seen a case acutely, and certainly never one in an adult.

She started to retch. She tried to gulp it back with an audible struggle.

I waited, and she managed to calm it down after a minute. I tried to show sympathy with my eyes. "That must feel awful. Let me order some medication and talk to the surgeon on call right away."

Now we had two A cases for the OR, but would Dr. Vrac take either of them?

35

DECEMBER 22, 11:30

GORDON

"Cost you extra over the holidays," Jim, not Jimmy, Stanton had told him.

Gordon flinched, calculating his student debt, but Dr. Vrac's face flashed in his mind. He'd spend anything to stop this man. "I'll cover it."

"My usual hourly rate's $70 an hour, but it's time-and-a-half over Christmas. Double on Christmas, Christmas Eve, New Year's Eve, and New Year's."

"Fine," said Gordon, punching the numbers in his calculator app.

"Flat rate of $250 for a full background check. I need a $1500 retainer. I'll send it all by email."

"All right." The $1500 would hurt, especially at this time of year. Gordon couldn't resist asking, "Are you related to the high school principal, Ms. Cortese?"

Jim Stanton snorted. "You really want to know?"

"No." Not at a rate of $105 to $140 per hour.

"Then sit tight, read through my email and sign the papers, and send me the retainer. Etransfer's fine. I'll be in touch when I got something for you."

After that etransfer, Gordon couldn't afford to fly back to Prince Edward

Island for Christmas. He didn't want to face his parents and the neighbours' questions anyway. He chose to work, hoping to operate with Dr. Vrac and Dr. Burns again, but the latter didn't appear on any OR lists over the holidays.

"He went to St. Joe's," said the charge nurse, looking vaguely surprised when Gordon asked.

"He switched hospitals?" Don't swim with the sharks, *Dr. Burns had said.*

"He ramped down over the past month or so. He couldn't leave outright because we needed him here." She pressed her lips together. "We still do. Dr. Q will go on maternity leave soon."

"I'm sorry to hear that," said Gordon, his stomach hollow. Dr. Burns had never given him his contact information. How would he follow up now?

36

MAY 22, 15:00

HOPE

"Put an NG tube down her," Cheng told me over the phone.

"Okay." I can do a nasogastric tube. "Will that actually make her stomach detort?"

"Maybe not, but it'll decompress the stomach and then it might reduce itself while I talk to Singh and Vrac."

"And the trauma?" Would the Vrac Attack accept him?

He paused. "I already talked to him about bed B."

"And?"

Cheng sighed. "He refused the consult."

"What?"

"He's probably yelling at Dr. Chia as we speak."

"Is that allowed?" I whispered into the receiver.

"I've never seen it before, but I've never worked with Dr. Vrac either. He marches to the beat of his own drum."

"He does something," I agreed. Something unrepeatable. And if Vrac hadn't already refused directly, I was the lucky winner who'd break the news to Dr. Chia.

On cue, Dr. Chia delivered a few choice words into her phone. Cathleen whispered "Vrac" to another nurse, who rolled her eyes.

This guy was infamous. Why did we all tolerate him?

Because that's what you do in medicine. You listen to your higher-ups, like in the army. You don't get a choice.

I couldn't take the trauma to the OR myself, and if I did, I wouldn't know what to do. Singh might know, but he didn't have permission to operate independently. Only Dr. Vrac did, and he ain't playing.

I swore to myself and belatedly realized I was still holding the phone. "Sorry."

"Agreed," said Cheng. "You need help with the NG tube?"

"I've done one before."

"Nebulized lidocaine," he said, telling me how to give pain control to make the procedure easier for the patient. "You can also try intranasal Fentanyl, but St. Joe's doesn't have the atomizers."

"Of course we don't," I muttered to myself.

He laughed. "See one, do one, teach one. Call me if you need help."

Watch a procedure, do it once, and then you're an expert. At the bigger teaching hospitals, that doesn't happen so much nowadays. Learners fight over procedures plus practice on mannequins in sim (simulation) labs instead.

Since I didn't want to bug Cheng or Singh, and they wanted to give me autonomy, it was show time.

"Need help?" asked Roxanne, and I turned to her gratefully. Nurses can do NG tubes without us.

The anatomy isn't hard. What's hard is that patients hate them. They're painful. You can imagine how good it feels to have a tube shoved through your nostril, down your throat, and into your stomach.

"NG tube," I told her.

"Bed 5, huh?" She nodded wisely. "Okay. No problem."

"Yeah?"

"I'll 'assist' you.'" She winked at me.

We both knew that meant she'd take over if needed. "You are the best," I said.

"Bring me a box of doughnuts next time."

"I will." I paused. "I didn't even know you liked doughnuts."

"They're okay. I pass them around to cheer everyone up, and they're cheap. I know I make more money than you."

"True story."

As she spoke, she gathered up the equipment one-handed. I followed, silently offering to carry it, so she dumped everything in my arms. "And we need gloves."

"Can we nebulize lidocaine first?"

"Yup, we just need to stop by this cart." She led me to the one across from the psych room and squatted to scoop the lidocaine from the bottom tray. "Keeps me in shape," she told me. "I get over 10,000 steps a day running around the ER."

"I bet." I get half those steps because I'm always charting. In my head, I rehearsed the best way to warn her that Vrac might grab her butt. "So Vrac is coming—"

"Ready! Did you put in the order for the nebulized lidocaine?" she asked.

"Uh, no." I hurried to a computer to fight to order it on our useless, expensive electronic medical records system, SARKET. The powers that be are like, *Well, we already paid millions of dollars for it, so just try and use it as best you can.*

I joined Roxanne at bed 5, where she'd started the nebulizer. "It'll be done in another few minutes," Roxanne assured me, and told the patient, "You'll see. It's better with the freezing. Breathe it all in. There you go."

"—STUPID FUCKS!" a man's thin voice hollered from the ambulance doors.

I flinched. Ms. Wells' eyes widened, so she'd heard it too.

Roxanne maintained her famous smile. "Ah. Our surgeon has arrived. Maybe he can take a look at you while he's here."

It seemed awfully quick for Vrac to show up, but it definitely sounded like him shouting through the thin curtain, "I said no and I mean no! That's what all you feminazis are always complaining about, right? No means no! Why can't you 'respect my autonomy' and the fact that I'm not operating on a trauma? I'm not even consulting on him. He is not my patient. Got that?"

"As his attending physician—" Dr. Chia said.

"Yeah! *You're* the attending, so *you* deal with it! There are surgeons at other hospitals, for Christ's sake. Trauma hospitals! Did you try UC?"

I heard the anger in Dr. Chia's low reply, even if I couldn't make out her actual words.

"What's this? Christ! Another consult. Are you a fucking consultologist? Did you not learn medicine in China, so you have to dump every patient on another service?"

My eyes widened. Dr. Chia was as Canadian as I was, not that either of us would be allowed to touch a maple leaf flag if Vrac had anything to do with it.

"Excuse me." Roxanne ducked out of the curtained room, and I gestured at Ms. Wells that I'd be back soon.

"—racist," said Dr. Chia quietly, as we approached. A male nurse and a security guard had joined their "conversation" near the ambulance entrance.

"Racist? How is your incompetence classified as racism? Don't you play the race card at me!" Dr. Vrac jabbed his finger at Dr. Chia's face.

"I'll report you," she said.

"Yeah? Better men than you have tried! And failed! Every time!"

"I'm not a man." Roxanne sidled up to Dr. Vrac as she spoke. Roxanne is a pretty, slim woman about my age and height with wavy brown hair and a 200 Watt smile. You can't help but like her. I'd never seen her get so close to the man—I hadn't had a chance to tell her to stay out of arm's reach—but she winked at Dr. Chia before she faced Vrac full on.

Dr. Vrac stared down at her. "Yeah? Who are you?"

"I'm Roxanne, your favourite ER nurse. You don't remember me?" She gazed up at him from under her eyelashes.

"Oh. Yeah. Roxanne." He obviously wanted to keep hurling racist, sexist epithets at Dr. Chia, but Roxanne's charms also beckoned. Dr.

Vrac's head ping-ponged between the two of them. "You're the Italian one, right?"

I choked and tried to hide it.

"I make the best pasta," Roxanne agreed, flipping her hair over her shoulder—she'd been wearing a small pony tail before, but she must've slipped off her hair tie so she could flirt with him. This was not Roxanne's first Vrac rodeo.

"You've only got one arm, though," Vrac pointed out. "Kind of useless."

I sucked in my breath. Dr. Chia opened her mouth. Roxanne beat us all to it.

"You'd be amazed what I can do with one hand, though. I'm *very* talented," she purred.

Wow. I'd never seen Roxanne like this. I'm always startled when residents dress up for the Christmas party and I realize that I work with very good-looking people. But Roxanne turned it on within seconds, and only by shaking her hair and standing differently.

Vrac crowed with laughter. "Haw! Haw! Haw!"

Dr. Chia and I shared a quick glance of amazement.

"Now, I know you want the best for patient care, just like we do," said Roxanne, holding his gaze with her soulful brown eyes.

"Sure."

"So I have a consult for you in bed 5. Gastric volvulus."

"Yeah? That's unusual."

"Very unusual. And I know we can use your expertise on B."

"We're not a trauma hospital," he said, but with much less conviction than before.

"It's such a shame. Good thing we have you as the closest thing to a trauma surgeon. Don't we?"

"Yeah," he growled.

"Come with me to bed B," she tossed over her shoulder as she undulated toward the trauma case.

"Careful," I muttered under my breath.

"You should transfer him to UC," he said half-heartedly, his eyes glued to her bum.

"We tried." Roxanne winked at him. "No beds."

"That's not my problem." But Vrac followed, and I beat it back to Ms. Wells in bed 5.

Her lidocaine finished up, spitting droplets instead of misting. With or without Roxanne, I'd place that NG tube even if Vrac ripped it out afterward. On surgery, delay meant weakness.

I picked up the NG tube and forced a smile at Ms. Wells. "We need to decompress your stomach. If it's twisted because it's too full of air, this will bring down the pain and help shift it back into place."

She nodded weakly.

I explained how I'd use a lot of lubricant and gently push the tube down her nose and eventually into her stomach.

She squeezed her eyes shut.

Vrac yanked back the curtain, the rings rattling on the rod. I tried not to gasp. My voice only trembled a little as I continued. "The tube hurts. I'm sorry about that. But the good news is, this would be your first step toward feeling better, and it could save you an operation."

She nodded again.

"Do you have any questions?"

She shook her head, eyes still closed and therefore shielded from Vrac.

I still hadn't heard her speak, but she understood. I squeezed her hand. After a beat, she squeezed back.

I shut off the nebulizer, greased up the NG tube generously, and approached Ms. Wells's nose. "Have you ever broken your nose before, or had nasal surgery?"

Her eyes blinked a no.

"That's good. I'll start with your right nostril. Statistically, it's a little bigger." I smiled as reassuringly as possible and began.

She moaned low in her throat.

"I'm sorry. Try to swallow as I advance the tube, and it'll go down easier." It takes quite a length of tube before we hit the nasopharynx (junction between the nose and throat) and esophagus, let alone the stomach.

She gargled with pain.

"Almost there," I said. "I see you. I hear you. I've got you." Roxanne asked patients to play their music on their phones to distract them. Too late for that now. "Think about something good. Like, do you like going to the beach? Or a fancy restaurant?"

She squeezed her eyelids shut.

I cast through my mind and seized on Tori's ghost. "A motorcycle?"

Her eyes flew open in surprise. She gave a faint nod. Vrac watched us, eyes gleaming.

"Okay, how about this. You're on your favourite bike, coasting along the road with no one else in sight, between the mountain and the ocean. Paradise." I hit the tube's three quarter mark. "The Maritimes."

Her mouth twitched, maybe not with pain this time.

"Oh, right. Not so many mountains out east. So let's say beautiful British Columbia. You and the open road between the Rockies and the Pacific Ocean ... "

Tori's ghost had slammed into something and died.

Goosebumps pebbled my skin. I steered away from that memory and finished the NG tube.

Fetid air whooshed out of the tube toward me.

I tried not to gag and grabbed the Toomey syringe, the real big 60 cc one, and uncapped it so I could attach it to the port on the side. You're supposed to inject air and listen at the stomach, but I had to fumble for my stethoscope and place it first. *Real cool, Hope.*

"What the fuck are you doing?" shouted Vrac.

Ms. Wells's eyes and mouth flew open.

I nearly dropped the syringe, but managed to catch it. "Checking the placement of the NG tube."

"Did you hear anything?" He meant air in the stomach.

"I was about to withdraw." I needed a second to pull back on the plunger and add air to the syringe before I attached it.

"So do it! Jesus Christ."

I exhaled and withdrew the stopcock of the syringe, using one hand to steady the body and the other to draw back the plunger.

"Is that how you handle a big one?" he asked, with a greasy grin.

Ooooh boy. I glanced at Ms. Wells, who gazed at Dr. Vrac, then at me.

He ignored her. "You should be able to work one-handed. You see that nurse, Rosie or whatever? Look what she can do with one hand. When you got one that good, you don't need two."

I felt myself reddening. Roxanne would have laughed him off, but I couldn't. One-handed syringe manoeuvres take hand strength and practice.

"As long as you're on my service, you'll get *lots* of hands-on time. All the practice you need." His gaze raked me up and down, seeming to penetrate my scrubs.

Tears of embarrassment stung my eyes. Dr. Chia faced him down and Roxanne fearlessly manipulated him into doing consults he'd already refused. Meanwhile, I felt humiliated.

You can do this, Hope. Don't let him win.

I pushed the Toomey plunger and heard air. I'd gotten the NG in.

"Give me that." Vrac snatched my stethoscope before I'd realized what he was doing. The tubing tangled in my hair, and while I reached up, Vrac stroked the nape of my neck, one quick finger touch down the length of it.

I suppressed a shout.

"You're a screamer, are you? I like that. Keeps things more interesting." His hands had transferred to the stethoscope, which he placed on Ms. Wells' left upper quadrant.

My eyes darted toward Ms. Wells. She regarded him with revulsion. She understood exactly what had happened.

Vrac ignored her disgust and my rage to manipulate the Toomey syringe. He drew back the stopcock with his thumb. "You see this? It's all in the thumb. I've got some items you can practice on. Come to my office after this."

No way in hell I'd go to his office willingly, especially not alone.

"I can't have a woman with bad hands on my team. Got to have good hands. Don't worry, I'll coach you. Now get this woman prepped. I'll take her for endoscopy after the appy."

He strode out to operate on the appendix, or B case, prioritizing it ahead of the two A cases at risk of imminent death.

37

MAY 22, 15:17

HOPE

At the computer, I tried to click the right items to get Ms. Wells set up for the OR.

Good news: he'll take care of one of our patients.

Bad news: he wants to give me "private lessons" in his office.

What should I do? Who could I tell?

"It's on this screen," said Singh, who'd appeared beside me.

"Oh! Thanks!" I said too loudly. He coached me through the clicks, but I wouldn't remember any of it.

Sexual harassment will do that to you. I've endured comments and touches outside the hospital, but not repeatedly from my own supervisor.

I felt pulled in a quadrillion directions. Who had tried to kill Dr. Burns? Who hit Mireille? How could I escape the angriest man alive yet still pass this rotation?

"You okay?" asked Singh.

After a minute, I shook my head.

"I know," he said.

Neither of us looked at each other. Then I burst out, "How can you stand it?"

His lips quivered. His eventual smile appeared with such a dead look in his eyes that I turned away again.

"I'm almost done," he said, like a mantra. He was heart-stoppingly close to finishing his five years of general surgery residency and getting the H-E-double hockey sticks out of here.

I pictured even five months with a man who'd started breaking my spirit within hours. My brain balked.

"You're a superstar," I said, and my voice broke.

He almost laughed. "If I were, I wouldn't be at this hospital."

That made me pause. "Don't general surgery residents come to St. Joe's?"

"Not in their last year."

Right. Why place your most experienced and skilled residents at a tiny, barely-part-of-the-teaching-circuit hospital, with no trauma, no transplants, no advanced cancer patients?

"What happened?" I whispered.

Singh made it simple. "He got shuffled here and he asked for me."

"Why?"

Singh shook his head instead of answering. Who knows why a madman does anything? He gazed at the patient in front of us, the one sitting up in his bed in front of the Plexiglas nursing station. "They were short here. The surgery resident went on mat leave. He said he needed the most experienced resident, and it would only be for a month."

"How long have you been here?"

"Two months. He made me transfer even before he got here himself. And I worked at UC with him nine months ago."

Creepy. Before I could ask more, Singh's pager beeped. "Let's go."

"Where?"

"To the OR. Appy's on the table, then the A case."

"Which A case?" I glanced at Ms. Wells's bed. I would have said the trauma patient came first, but no one was asking me. And I guess it was better to have one life-saving surgery than none.

"You can scrub in," Singh offered.

I smiled anemically. This whole morning, I'd been looking

forward to it. Now I didn't want to stand next to Vrac in case he rubbed against me, in addition to poisoning the air with his words.

"See you in OR 3."

"For sure. Could I ask you a question? About, uh, a case at UC?" My heart fluttered. Nikki had said he was named in the lawsuit.

Singh's shoulders stiffened. All expression drained from his face. "I have nothing to say about that."

"I'm sorry. I didn't mean—" He'd held out an olive branch to me, and I'd torched it.

He walked away without a word, the ER door swinging closed behind him.

38

JAN 6, 09:35

GORDON

At least Jim didn't waste time. "I got something. You want me to wait and type up a report, or send things as I find 'em?"

"Send them." Gordon couldn't sleep anyway.

Obituary of Mike Vrac

The world lost Mike suddenly on Saturday morning, as a result of a tragic motorcycle accident ...

Gordon checked the top of the obituary and calculated the dates. Mike had only been 16 years old and "Waldo" 17½.

For the first time, Gordon felt something like empathy for Vlad Vrac.

"Is this it?" Gordon asked the empty room. "Is this what warped you your entire life?"

39

MAY 22, 18:33

HOPE

"Doesn't look good, man," said Cheng, as I entered OR 3. I'd run the wards and missed the appy, which meant I hadn't scrubbed in for a single surgery yet.

"Which part?" I asked.

"This patient," Cheng said, pointing to the man on the table.

I flinched at the now-greyish cast to the man's face, but at least they'd taken the trauma patient from room B. Finally. Even though I worried about Ms. Wells too.

"I'm working on it," said the female anesthetist, pointing at the monitor and the bags of blood.

"Non-operative management, Dr. Nanut," said Dr. Vrac, sweeping into the room with his hands already scrubbed. The scrub nurse brought him his gown and tied it. He inserted his hands into the sterile gloves she held for him, one hand at a time, as he spoke. "He's a grade III splenic lac anyway. What's the harm?"

"Hemodynamic instability and death," Dr. Nanut replied. In other words, shock and death as the blood poured out of the cut in his spleen.

Vrac cackled while Singh said something about an open approach "because we won't be able to suction fast enough."

"I can suck more any day of the week!" Vrac shouted.

"There's also pneumoperitoneum," said Dr. Nanut. "Laparoscopy compresses the inferior vena cava, impairing preload. As you know —" Her tone said that he had no clue—"the IVC is the major vein that returns blood to the heart from the lower body."

Translation: when you add CO2 to the belly during your surgery, it flattens the veins. Even less blood returns to the heart. The patient's circulation will collapse even if you do manage to suction the blood fast enough, you dumbass.

"Well, I guess that's why you get paid the big bucks," Vrac replied. "You keep the patient's blood pressure up, and I'll decide if I want to open the belly. For now, it's a closed case. Case closed." He chuckled.

No one else did. Both Singh and anesthesia wanted to open the patient's belly. Now.

The circulating nurse held up the landline receiver covered with a sterile green towel. "Phone for you."

She held it up to Vrac's ear while he bawled, "Why you calling me again? You fix it or not?"

I glanced at the patient's vitals: blood pressure 93/45, heart rate 122 even with anesthesia titrating blood and pressors, which meant he'd already bled way too much. Dr. Nanut and I shared a look.

Hemodynamic instability and death.

I'd put my money on Drs. Singh and Nanut any day of the week, but neither of them had the authority to override this dreadful man.

"You want me to rent a fuckin' BIXI?" shouted Dr. Vrac into the receiver.

I snorted to myself. BIXI rents out bikes in Montreal. It's actually really convenient to rent a bike in one spot, use it, and "return" it at your destination.

"You fix it. That's why I pay you the big bucks!" Dr. Vrac laughed, finally walking away from the phone to crane his neck at the patient's vitals. "Can't figure out how to stabilize him, eh, Numb Nuts?"

I bit back a gasp. I'd never seen a surgeon insult anesthesia like this.

"I beg your pardon," said Dr. Nanut, ice dripping from every word, as she swiftly inserted a line in the internal jugular vein.

"That's your name, isn't it?" Vrac made an elaborate face. "Oh, Dr. Na*nut.* My bad."

"This patient requires an urgent splenectomy with an open approach," she replied.

"Who died and made you a board-certified trauma surgeon?"

Cheng murmured to me, changing the subject, "Can you define a grade III splenic laceration?"

"Grade I is the least injured and grade V is the worst," I whispered back.

Vrac swung around to stare at us. "Well, look who wins a cookie today! The little lady knows which way splenic laceration gradations go! Next you'll figure out how to tie your shoes!"

Cheng cast me an apologetic look.

I squared my shoulders and faced Dr. Vrac. He'd stopped picking on Dr. Nanut, allowing the woman to issue massive transfusions in relative peace. I secretly sent a prayer to Dr. Burns. *You helped me out this morning. Now I'm returning the favour to one of your colleagues.*

"It's not that hard, girlie. You need a minute to look it up on your phone?"

"Not necessary. Grade I to III all involve subcapsular hematomas, IV involves a vascular injury, and V is a shattered spleen."

Singh silently backed open the door, his arms held in the air so he didn't contaminate his hands. The scrub nurse met him with his gown.

Vrac looked like he'd been forced to chug his own vomit. He spat at me, "You should have a more detailed breakdown on grade I to III. It's not as if they're all the same. That's why we have three different grades!"

Cheng quietly held out ten fingers, confirming what I already knew before I answered. "Grade I is a subcapsular hematoma less than 10 percent of the surface area."

"Yeah? What about parenchymal lacerations?"

That, I hadn't remembered, but Singh held his index and thumb a centimetre apart for a second in my peripheral vision, so I said confidently, "One centimetre."

"Or less! Jesus." But he turned away from me and snapped at the anesthetist, "Are you ready, Numb Nuts? You don't want this man to die on you, do you?"

I exhaled. I'd managed to take the heat for what, a minute?

But the small crinkle around Dr. Nanut's eyes told me that she'd noticed.

Time to scrub in. I headed for the sinks outside the OR, ten steps behind Cheng. When I returned, Vrac would quiz me on the anatomy, which isn't necessarily easy to figure out with a keyhole view. While I cleaned my nails, I reviewed landmarks in my head.

As I re-entered the darkened room, I kept my hands in the air at upper chest level and checked the metal Mayo stand for a self-serve gown and gloves. The tray's empty metal surface gleamed back at me. They'd forgotten me.

"Hi," I said to the circulating nurse, the one who moves around the room and handles the non-sterile instruments. I glanced at her badge. "Brooke?"

Brooke strode toward the OR table without a glance at me.

Dr. Vrac stood at the patient's side with Singh beside him and Cheng opposite him. "Ready, gentlemen?"

I cleared my throat. "Not ready."

Cheng kept his back to me. Singh didn't look up. Brooke kept her eyes trained on them, completely ignoring me.

"Excuse me?" I tried again.

As if I hadn't spoken, Singh made his incision and Cheng slid in the trocar, the sharp but hollow instrument that would allow them to place the laparoscopic ports.

"Careful now. We don't want a repeat!" Vrac snapped.

"Slow and steady," said Cheng. "I've never had any complaints." *In the bedroom*, his tone implied, making Vrac snort and defusing the tension.

"Belly up," said Vrac.

Six feet away from the table, I watched the belly inflate with CO2. But what about me operating? I couldn't miss my first surgery of the whole rotation. I said louder, "Excuse me."

Brooke offered an instrument to the scrub nurse.

"Could I have gloves and a gown? Please?" My voice rang throughout the room, but no one turned. Vrac must have ordered them to ignore me, and ignore me they did, as effectively as if I'd died.

Singh handed Cheng the laparoscope, or camera, to project the organs on the screen.

"Blood and bubbles," Vrac said in disgust. "Switch to a Veress needle."

"We need to open," said Singh.

"Veress needle," Vrac repeated.

I heard the OR door swing open and swivelled to face it, my hands still carefully raised in the air. If I touched too low on my own chest, I'd contaminate myself, and they'd have good reason to kick me out.

Tammy, the charge nurse, frowned at me from the doorway.

"Could you please help me with a sterile gown and gloves?" I asked her quietly. "There's nothing on the stand. I don't mind grabbing them and rescrubbing if you show me where they are."

Tammy shook her head. My stomach plummeted even before she asked, "Did he say you could scrub in?"

I glanced at the surgical team suctioning frank blood out of the abdomen. Bright red blood meant he was bleeding faster now. "I spoke to the residents—"

"Not the residents. Did *Dr. Vrac* say you could scrub in?" She enunciated each word like I was a Deaf foreigner.

I flinched. "I didn't have a chance to ask him personally."

"You need his express permission to scrub into his OR. He runs a tight ship."

"So I should ... observe?"

Her eyes narrowed. "Do whatever you need to do to make his life easier. That's your job."

I opened my mouth to object before I closed it again. Everyone said the charge nurse ran the whole operating section. I couldn't get on her bad side too.

"You're the lowest cockroach on the totem pole. Get used to it." She exited the room.

I watched the door flap closed behind her, disbelieving. Should I keep standing here the entire case with my hands in the air, or give up?

"Dr. Snooze." Vrac's voice snapped through the air.

That's not my name either. I ground my teeth but made my way to his side. "Yes." I refused to add *sir.*

"Did you hear what the charge nurse told you?"

He didn't bother looking at me. His eyes fixed on the screen as he suctioned burgundy blood that now looked a bit watery. Maybe they'd irrigated it with water so it wouldn't clog up their tubes.

I continued to hold up my arms, which had started to go numb. "Yes."

"She's exactly right. Your job is to do whatever I need to make my life easier. *Capice?"*

I nodded dumbly.

"Say yes, sir or no, sir."

I'd break a molar grinding my teeth if he kept this up. Cheng's eyes flashed sympathetically above his surgical mask as he worked, but he didn't speak or maintain eye contact.

"Yes, sir," I mumbled.

"Tammy's a good nurse. Decades of experience. None of this 'me too' nonsense."

At least he'd heard of the #metoo campaign to raise awareness of men sexually harassing women. I nodded and belatedly added, "Yes, sir."

"You should be more like Tammy. Why don't you follow her around?"

I raised my eyes over the patient's still body. Tammy had reopened the door and now hovered in the doorway, watching us.

"I don't understand. Sir."

"You're not a surgeon. You'd be better off as a charge nurse. Get out of my sight and follow Tammy instead."

40

JANUARY 7, 13:54

GORDON

Gordon didn't consider Mikhail's tragic death the whole story. "Waldo" had sought a punishing schedule since high school. What about the absent mother?

"Patience," said Jim. "I'll get what you need. You know what they call me?"

"No."

"The last stand. Because my last name's Stanton, see? I'm a rock. I don't give up."

Gordon's shoulders sagged in relief. He could use a rock to clear his name and move Vrac into retirement land.

"Now, I can't find much on the mother, Nadia Smith. You sure that's her name?"

Irritation pricked the skin of Gordon's forehead. "That's what's in the paper I sent you."

Jim paused before he answered. It sounded like he thumbed a lighter for a cigarette. "That's what she told 'em. That don't mean it's her name."

"Wouldn't she show ID when she applied for Canadian citizenship?" Gordon had no idea. He'd never helped anyone apply.

"Leave it to me," said Jim.

41

MAY 22, 18:54

HOPE

I remained beside Vrac, cemented in shock.

Once an emergency doctor had yelled at Tucker as a med student, "I don't have time for you! Go stand against the wall!"

Still, that doctor hadn't ordered Tucker to switch to nursing instead. They're different skill sets. I'd already sunk over $200,000 in debt for a medical education, so I know how to diagnose, intubate, install central lines, run a code, and run a floor.

But I hardly ever start IVs or attach patients to a cardiac monitor, I don't know how to run medications through pumps, or even basic things like transferring a patient to a chair without hurting both of us. As for Tammy's skill set, I don't do scheduling at all, let alone for a set of operating rooms.

Tammy glowered at me while I stood stock still.

"You want to fail the rotation for disobeying me?" Vrac's voice dropped dangerously low.

"No, of course not," I managed.

Vrac's eyes flickered with satisfaction before he turned back to his monitor and the surgery at hand.

"Come on, then," said Tammy, clearly disgusted.

I turned to follow her out, still holding my arms in the air, keeping them sterile. I couldn't give up. I've always been a "wait until the fat lady sings" kind of person, and I refused to dangle my arms by my sides and contaminate them until we hit the door.

Someone made a choked noise.

I pivoted in time to see Singh shout from behind his mask. "What are you—*no!*"

Bright red arterial blood splashed the screen, obscuring everyone's view.

Alarms sounded on the anesthesia machines. Dr. Nanut swore.

"What did you do?" Vrac called to Singh.

"I didn't—" Singh protested.

Cheng cut in. "Convert to open."

"Towel," called Vrac.

The circulating nurse instantly ported him a sterile green towel. Dr. Vrac seized it and tossed it on Singh's head, shrouding his face.

Singh instinctively jerked his head back, trying to shake the material off without using his hands, but first Vrac punched Singh's face through the towel.

We all heard the soft crunch as his nasal bones fractured.

Singh gargled from behind the towel. Burgundy blood flooded a river down the green fabric.

Vrac had already turned back to the patient. "Ten blade," he said to the scrub nurse, holding out his hand for the scalpel.

While the scrub nurse bleated in shock, Vrac grabbed the scalpel off the tray himself and sliced open the patient's abdomen from xiphoid to pubis.

42

MAY 22, 19:00

HOPE

Blood. So much blood.

Singh yelled something I couldn't make out as he now used the sterile towel to staunch the blood flowing from both his nostrils.

"All four quadrants?" Cheng demanded, so he must have understood Singh.

"Pack 'em!" Singh commanded in a nasal voice, and I realized that the senior resident had contaminated his gloves with the towel saturated with his own blood, but now issued instructions to his junior resident to save the man's life.

"No one moves unless I say," Vrac intoned, seemingly unperturbed by the patient's blood waterfalling down the drape, onto his legs and clogs.

" ... ruptured the spleen!" Singh shouted.

"Unless I say," Vrac repeated, and both residents stopped dead.

"I need to resuscitate him!" Dr. Nanut snapped.

"Fuck you," said Vrac.

I stood frozen with my hands still in midair.

Vrac and Tammy had both ordered me to do nothing unless expressly given permission by the attending surgeon.

No CPR?

No code?

Should I watch this young man die over a surgeon's ego?

I ventured toward the code bell as unobtrusively as possible. A simple white string hung from it, making it easy to pull. I snuck my hand toward it.

"No, fuck YOU," said Dr. Nanut, and beat me to the code string. She yanked it so hard that she snapped it off.

"You'll never work with me again!" Vrac stomped over to yell in her face.

"Fine with me," she told him. "I doubt you'll work much after this," she added under her breath, adding a pressure bag to squeeze the blood in faster.

"What's happening?" called a white man from the doorway. I recognized him from the code this morning.

"Code Omega on a ruptured spleen," Dr. Nanut snapped. "BP 60 over palp. I need all hands on deck here."

I stepped toward her. Palp meant his blood pressure had sunk so low, she could no longer measure the second number, only palpate it (detect it by touch).

"NO ONE MOVES UNLESS I SAY!" Vrac screamed, his elbows swinging. Singh stayed clear this time, but Cheng had leaned toward the scrub nurse's tray for more sponges.

Vrac slammed Cheng in the gut.

Cheng buckled over with a gasp. A sponge slipped out of his hand and plopped into the open abdominal cavity.

The scrub nurse bit back a scream.

"I knock 'em over like ninepins! I do Crossfit! Stay the fuck away unless you want more of this!" Vrac shouted, balling both fists in the air.

Tammy returned, pushing ahead of the growing crowd of helpers who didn't dare advance into the room as Vrac bobbed and weaved with an imaginary enemy.

"That's enough," Tammy told him.

"Shut up, Tammy!"

"No, you shut up," she said, with such contempt that he withered momentarily. "Are you going to save that man's life, or aren't you?"

Vrac glanced down at the man's abdomen, which spewed blood while Cheng gasped for air. "We're packing him."

"Then do it," Tammy said, shoving her way past the crowd back into the hallway.

"I didn't call you!" Vrac yelled at her back. "I didn't call any of you!" he bawled at the others clustered in the doorway. I recognized the med student from this morning, Greg, his eyes wide above his surgical mask.

Singh applied pressure to his own nose. Cheng held the draped edge of the OR table as he audibly sucked in his breath. At least he could breathe again.

"Pussy," said Vrac, hip checking Cheng, who stumbled into the anesthesia machine. Cheng caught himself on the machine in a quick recovery that contaminated his gloves.

My mouth dropped open behind my mask. Now neither senior residents could touch the patient without rescrubbing.

A rustle from Brooke caught my eye. She'd laid out sterile size six gloves and a gown on the Mayo tray without a word.

Now suited up, I darted to the operating table, seizing the remaining sponges from the tray.

"What are you doing?" screamed Vrac.

"Packing all four quadrants!" I hit the left upper quadrant first (LUQ), home of the spleen, shoving in clean sponges that instantly darkened, saturated in blood.

Singh called something from behind his towel, which my brain took a second to translate as "Apply pressure."

"Get away from there, you stupid cunt!" Vrac bawled.

I thrust extra sponges in the LUQ. Blood spouted over my gloved fingers. When Vrac swung at me, I had to duck. More blood gushed from the belly.

Vrac hurled himself around the table at me. I abandoned position so I could circle the table myself, now facing the people in the hallway.

"Don't you fuckin' touch that patient," said Vrac. "Touching a patient without consent, that's physical assault."

"I'm sure the *patient* gives consent. You're not his power of attorney," I mumbled the last bit since he could outright fail me in front of a dozen people.

"Do you need help?" asked a woman whose dark hair escaped her scrub cap.

"I need help here!" called Dr. Nanut. She alone had kept working silently, steadily. She glanced at the frozen crowd. "I activated the MTP already"—Mass Transfusion Protocol, I mentally translated—"but I need 1:1:1:1, I need calcium, tranexamic acid—"

"Don't you fucking move," Vrac told the mass of bodies before they could run for red blood cells and the rest.

"You are legally responsible if this man dies," Dr. Nanut threw at him.

"So what's another lawsuit?" Vrac replied.

I seized the sponges again.

"Insubordination! Inability to understand direct orders! Immediate fail. You're off my service with no right to interfere with a single case. Get the fuck out of here!"

Singh watched me gravely from above his bloody towel as I slowly withdrew my hands.

Dr. Nanut swore. I could smell her sweat. "I need help!"

No one else stirred.

"Get out of here, Sze! I don't want you within ten feet of this fucking patient, you little bitch!"

I couldn't stay. I couldn't leave. I let him focus his ire on me while Cheng quietly took over packing, until Vrac lunged at me.

We all gasped while I retreated halfway to the door.

"All the way out, bitch! You want me to break your nose, too?"

43

JANUARY 9, 08:32

GORDON

Jim emailed a series of documents that Gordon had to page through before he called him back. "Her name wasn't Nadia Smith?"

"She did marry a guy named Charlie Smith who died when the boys were 16 and 17," said Jim. He sounded like he was enjoying himself.

Gordon frowned. "You'd think she would have changed the boys' names to something easy like Smith."

"They weren't Charlie's sons. Nadezhda already had them in Russia before she made her way over here."

"What did you call her?" Gordon struggled with the pronunciation. His stutter made everything worse.

"Nadezhda Vasilyeva." Jim rolled the syllables.

"That doesn't sound like Vrac," said Gordon.

"No, Vrac was her first husband. Met him in France."

Gordon held his head. He'd never realized how a woman's identity could shift with every marriage, especially while changing countries pre-Internet. "He adopted both boys?"

"Got it in one. Can't figure out what happened to the first husband, but good old Charlie died a month after Mike."

"A month?"

"Twenty-eight days, to be precise."

Gordon scanned through the documents, but Jim cut in first. "Car accident."

"Motor vehicle collision." Gordon replied automatically with the medical term because an "accident" by an impaired driver or poor road design could have been prevented. "Isn't that a bit strange? The stepson died in a motorcycle crash, and then the stepfather dies in a car crash soon afterward?"

Jim sighed. "Civilians always jump to conclusions."

"Wh-what do you mean?"

"You think someone killed him, right?"

"I didn't say that."

"You were thinking it. Well, let me tell you, son, back then, they frowned on drinking and driving, but people did it. Seat belts didn't become mandatory in Saskatchewan until 1977, and not everyone obeyed. Cars weren't built the same back then. It's much more likely that Charlie was grieving his stepson and ended up taking a turn too fast."

"Far more likely," Gordon agreed, but the look on Dr. Vrac's face boiled inside him. "Still, can you look into Mike and Charlie's deaths?"

"Sure. It'll cost you."

"What about the retainer?"

"I've got it. I'll send you the bill for what was done so far, and you can decide if you want me to keep looking."

"Oh, I want you to," said Gordon. He could almost taste the victory. Maybe he stuttered. Maybe he could have run the code on Joan Finn better. But at long last, Gordon had grabbed Vrac by the short hairs, and he couldn't stop now.

44

MAY 22, 19:57

HOPE

Dr. Nanut finally declared the patient's time of death.

A dark-skinned woman turned away from OR 3 and headed down the hall, but not before I glimpsed the tears in her eyes above her mask.

None of us could speak afterward, except Dr. Nanut, who turned to face the remaining staff lingering in the doorway. "Trent Jones was only 29 years old." Then she stalked to the adjoining room, where we could hear her dictating, "Patient ID number AL000483799 ... "

"Fuck that. You need to dictate too," Dr. Vrac told Singh.

Singh gestured wordlessly at his bloody towel. He still applied pressure with his opposite hand.

Vrac snorted. "A nasal fracture is not a medical emergency. Get your work done first. Then you can whine to the emergency doctors about your modelling career."

First, do no harm, Hippocrates had written.

We had all done harm today. Vrac had bullied us into silence and inaction and beat both his residents into allowing a man to bleed to death.

"This ain't right," Andy muttered from the doorway.

"Who said that? Come here and say it to my face. I'll fucking cut you with this!" Vrac challenged the crowd with his 10 blade scalpel still wet with the patient's blood.

No one would believe this. I discarded my gloves, quietly reached into my pocket and started the video on my phone. I didn't dare hold it up to film him, but it would capture the audio.

"What's the matter, you never seen a patient die before? He had a splenic laceration, you twats! Get over it!" Vrac shouted. "You're not a trauma hospital. You're not used to seeing people die. Well, I am, you numb nuts! Get back to work!"

"We need to call a coroner," a Black woman replied.

"You don't call anyone until I say! Jesus Christ! Do I have to punch all of you in the face before you understand who's the boss around here? *There can only be one!"*

Singh hesitated before he started out of the room.

"Where the fuck do you think you're going, you monkey?"

"You asked me to dictate," Singh said, his voice still muffled under his towel.

"Oh, yeah, that's right. You better dictate it good. It's all on you. Who punctured that spleen?" Vrac glared at him until Singh turned away. "That's right, you fucking pussy. *You did."*

Cheng blinked and made an involuntary sound. His shoulders hunched, even though he no longer protected his midsection.

Singh crossed into the adjoining room. He picked up the black receiver to dictate, refusing to meet anyone else's eyes.

I turned away so as not to accentuate the humiliation.

Someone had once advised me, if you're going to go rogue, do it so completely that when other people describe it, no one will believe them.

Dr. Vrac had proven the point. I'd started recording so late that I'd missed the actual death and the assaults.

Even with up to ten people observing and potentially testifying against him, who would believe what Vrac had done?

Would anyone dare stand up to this rabid alpha dog? (Although I'd take a canine any day over Vrac, even a rabid one. They suffer from an infectious disease. I couldn't figure Vrac out beyond a severe antisocial personality and narcissism.)

The only people who'd defied this surgeon? Dr. Nanut and Tammy and, to a certain extent, me and Cheng. None of us had made a difference.

Singh would graduate July first. Why jeopardize his entire medical career when he'd break free in 6 weeks? Someone would set Singh's nose shortly, making it almost as good as new.

Cheng had basically told me "not my monkeys, not my circus." He'd head back to urology with a bunch of wild stories, forgetting about that one time he got punched in the stomach.

Everyone in that doorway needed to feed their families, which hinged on them keeping their mouths shut so they could work another day. I heard disapproving murmurs from the group, but no one stood up and demanded, *How could you?*

Then we'd have to face the question, *How could we?*

Cheng looked pale as he followed Singh to add his two cents to the dictation.

"Fill out the death certificate, Sneeze," Vrac tossed over his shoulder at me before he swanned out of OR 3 and the crowd parted before him. "Make yourself useful."

45

JANUARY 25, 15:45

GORDON

"I'll be damned," said Jim, as soon as Gordon picked up.

"What did you find?" Gordon could hardly speak over his heartbeat.

"D'you see the notes I emailed? I started with Mike's death and interviewing people around here who remembered it. Charlie was a carpenter. He didn't want to spend money on car service if he could help it, so he fixed the chain on Mike's motorcycle himself."

Gordon's breath hissed out between his teeth. "And then Mike died."

"And then Mike died," Jim agreed. "I couldn't get anyone to come out and sign anything about it, but they had theories. Charlie was a cheap bastard who probably reused a chain from a different model and didn't know how to tighten it right. No wonder it snapped when Mike turned a corner."

"We need proof," said Gordon.

"I don't know that you'll get any, but a lot of people had the same theory you did, about how it was a mighty coincidence that Charlie died right after Mike. They said that Waldo didn't sleep for that month, wouldn't take any time off school, wouldn't accept any help. Tried to return the casseroles they dropped off on their porch—they still remember that."

"And then?" Gordon knew the point wasn't casseroles.

"And then Charlie's car brakes failed. He crashed into a tree. Killed himself and his wife."

Gordon made a sound low in his throat.

"Waldo was supposed to go out with them. They were on their way to church. Trying to get back to normal after losing Mike. Waldo talked back, shouted at Charlie, and refused to go. Said he'd never get in a car with Charlie again. Shouted so loud that the neighbours heard it up and down the street. Charlie cuffed him and jumped into the car."

"And drove into the tree," said Gordon.

"Yup. Him and his wife. Firefighters, police, and ambulance came out, but no one could help them."

Gordon rubbed his head. "Waldo raised himself after that?"

"He graduated on time, and even made valedictorian." Jim didn't sound entirely approving. "Some folks still talk about that, but he's done well for himself, there's no denying that."

Gordon shook his head instead of trying to explain that "well" and Vrac didn't belong in the same postal code. "I need to think about this."

"You do that. You want me to write my report now?"

"No," said Gordon slowly. "Write up what you've got so far, but we're not done yet."

46

MAY 22, 20:07

HOPE

"The death certificate?" I asked Vrac's back.

He waved the back of his hand at me like he'd asked me to do his laundry and I should already know where he kept the detergent.

Vrac seemed allergic to paperwork of all kinds. On the upside, he no longer commanded me to follow Tammy around. But Vrac had deliberately let a patient die, assaulted 3 out of 3 residents physically or sexually within 12 hours, and verbally ambushed every biped.

I made my way to the dictation room, an olive green-tiled adjoining room attached to the OR with no door so you could wander in and out.

Up until now, in the rare event that a patient did pass away under our care, I'd watched the attending write the notes and dictate. They knew this case would be investigated and believed "the buck stops here."

Somehow, Vrac thought that not only that he could get away with killing this man in front of a dozen witnesses, but he could waltz away without sullying his hands with any paperwork.

The circulating nurse held out a piece of paper to me. Even at ten paces, I recognized the death certificate.

I shook my head. Vrac couldn't pawn everything off on us. He was the only one here with operating privileges, as he kept throwing in our faces.

Still, Vrac had gotten away with everything up until now. Why not murder?

The crowd murmured to each other. "Not right."

"He's crazy."

"We need to report this."

But they all spoke in low voices, as if their objections wouldn't last the hour.

I hadn't drunk the surgical Kool Aid. I could report his ass anytime. But would I?

"Take it." The circulating nurse flapped the death certificate at me in irritation before reaching for the closest IV in the patient's right arm.

I tucked the certificate under my arm. "This is a coroner's case." A few people in the doorway turned to listen. "You need to leave every tube as is." The family won't like the tube in the patient's mouth and IVs dangling from the skin, but you're not supposed to change anything until the coroner gives permission.

The circulating nurse's hand stilled while she glanced at the scrub nurse. They turned to the doorway, waiting for Dr. Vrac to return and tell them what to do.

Fortunately, he'd sailed off. I faced them. "I'm calling the coroner. This man is no longer Dr. Vrac's patient. The coroner could start an investigation at any moment. Removing an IV is considered removing evidence." I hurried into the dictation room, where Dr. Nanut hung up her black phone receiver and told me, "Don't bother. I'll call the coroner myself."

"Thank you. You're awesome," I said. She'd led the charge against Vrac. Still, I waited to make sure she'd follow through.

" ... a grade III splenic laceration. Dr. Vrac opted for a laparoscopic approach ... " Singh dictated.

I stood at the ledge that made a primitive desk, staring through the Plexiglas windows at the two nurses who spoke with their heads bent over the remains. Both Dr. Nanut and Dr. Singh stood as they dictated on their phones, and I didn't want to slip between them to claim the one stool when both of them deserved it far more than me. At least the circulating nurse had stopped trying to dismantle the evidence.

"The spleen was punctured by the trocar," Singh narrated.

I winced. News to me. No wonder the patient had crashed.

I logged into the closest computer. If I ended up filling out the death certificate for Trent Jones, I'd need his medical history.

Cheng joined us silently, and I asked, "Would you call the splenic puncture the cause of death? Or would you say the splenic laceration was a preceding condition, and—"

Cheng turned his dark eyes on me while Singh stopped dictating.

"You want my advice?" Cheng asked, dangerously soft.

I nodded.

"Don't fill out the death cert."

"Oh. But he said ... "

"I know," Cheng said, and pressed his lips together so firmly that I knew that was his last word on it.

Dr. Nanut began arguing with the locating department about how best to reach the coroner. "You should have a direct number. Who's the coroner on call? Call them now."

I smothered a nervous laugh. After hours, a security guard acted as the operator, so they were even more incompetent than usual.

I checked my phone for a direct number to the coroner's office, which I showed to Dr. Nanut. She hung up on locating and called that number.

What exactly had happened in this OR? Trent Jones had already suffered a cut to his spleen in the parking lot, as shown on CT, which meant he'd slowly bled while waiting for the OR. Then "the spleen was punctured by the trocar." Had Vrac accidentally or deliberately stabbed the man's spleen during the surgery itself before forcing us all to watch him die?

47

MAY 22, 20:25

HOPE

"Hi there," I called to Singh's back, following him out.

"There's a consult in emerg. Cholecystitis." Singh removed the towel, and his nose trickled blood, but less than before. He grimaced and pressed the towel back on.

"Right, but first could I ask you—"

"No. I've got to look after myself now."

Singh cut toward the door. He did need that nose looked at, but I kept pace so I could whisper in his ear, "Did Vrac puncture the spleen with the trocar?"

His shoulders jerked as if I'd shot him from behind, but he didn't answer me.

"Don't take the fall for it," I said. "Please."

Singh didn't turn around as he swiftly rounded the hallway and out of sight.

"Leave him alone," said another man's voice.

I jumped a little before I turned around to face Cheng. "I'm trying to protect him. Vrac wants—"

"I know what Vrac wants. *I* saw him do it."

"You saw him stab the spleen? Because if you'll testify about it—"

"I don't know what I'll do. I haven't decided." Cheng's voice brooked no argument. "Singh is in an abusive relationship, and you nagging him is not going to help him."

I set my teeth. "I'm not *nagging* him." What a sexist, gaslighting way of putting it. "I'm giving him permission to *break* that abusive relationship instead of letting the guy walk all over him."

"He's not asking you to. Go do the ER consult." Cheng checked his watch. "We don't have much time before the volvulus. I heard GI took her for a scope that didn't work."

I swore. Of course it didn't. Now Ms. Wells's life depended on an OR from the world's meanest surgeon while the chief resident headed to the ER for his own emergency. At least Cheng and I could still assist. Well, Cheng. I'd been fired.

"Think about it," I told Cheng, but my pager went off, undercutting my firm tone. I checked the pager display and recognized the extension from the ER. Cheng had already started walking away from me, but I couldn't resist one final shot. "You know the right thing to do."

Cheng whipped around. My stomach somersaulted. Cheng would make a dangerous enemy. He hadn't gotten into urology by chance. It goes beyond medical expertise and an easy personality. You must also "play the game" expertly, meaning you know whose ass to kiss, whose to leave alone with a smile, how to maximize your work ethic over here and appear effortless over there, and how and where to show off your research.

In addition to the THC gummy fiasco during medical school, I absolutely failed the game. Someone would have to manually explain to me who I needed to impress, how to do it, and why. I never instinctively understood how to charm every soul while extracting exactly what I wanted from each of them.

Exhibit A: at this very moment, I'd achieved the trifecta by infuriating both my senior residents as well as my evil overlord.

"If you want. I'm on my way to the ER," I added, too cheerfully.

"Good." Cheng's phone chimed, and both of us glanced at the caller ID: Delilah.

Cheng smiled for real as he answered the scrub nurse, "Hey, you."

I hurried down the stairs, marvelling at the progression. This morning, Cheng had expressed an interest in Delilah; by evening, she was calling him. Maybe she'd heard about Trent's death and wanted first-hand confirmation.

She could have called the other nurses for that, though. I heard affection and intimacy in those two words, *Hey, you.*

Back in the day, doctors and nurses hooked up all the time. Not as common now. Most of us don't care as much about roles so much, like my surgery resident friend dating a physiotherapist, but studies show that physicians are more likely to marry other physicians now that women outnumber men in med school.

Nurses often date other nurses. If you're a heterosexual male making up the 10 percent of the nursing population, you can often take your pick of beautiful, caring colleagues. Unlike doctors, you both get paid overtime, parental leave, and a pension.

"Still working?" called one of the patients lined up for admission in the hallways outside the ER. This woman looked half the others' ages, maybe in her 40s.

I nodded and gestured as the casts on both her arms. "Too bad."

"It is what it is." The patient glanced at one of her elderly neighbours who'd started banging on her bed railings.

I nodded and saluted her before I pushed open the doors to the ER. I opened the chart for the 48-year-old chole patient, read the ultrasound, and performed a not-very-impressive physical exam. Mild right upper quadrant pain with her cholecystitis (inflamed gall bladder), but no guarding or rebound.

"Can I go home?" she asked.

"Well, your white blood cell count is high. Can you rate your pain out of 10? Ten is someone ripping your leg off, one is almost nothing."

"I don't know, a three? Can I go home?" She checked her phone.

"I'll talk to my senior resident first."

"Oh, God. Then who are you?"

"I'm Dr. Sze, the junior resident."

She rolled her eyes. "Pul-leeze. I need to get out of here. I haven't eaten since last night! I'm dying!"

"I'll see what I can do." She looked ready for discharge, but one of my seniors could get hung up on her white count and her ultrasound. I refused to promise anything I couldn't deliver.

"Who's the surgeon on call?"

"Dr. Vrac."

She shot straight up in bed. "Get me out of here."

"Um—"

"That guy is *not* gonna touch me. He killed my aunt, Joan Finn. I thought he worked at UCH, so I came here."

I cleared my throat. "He did work at UCH, but he recently obtained privileges at St. Joe's."

She held up her arm. "Take out my IV."

I backed away from her. "Could you sign the 'leaving against medical advice' form first, knowing that you have an increased risk of infection, septic shock, and death if you leave before you've been fully assessed by the surgical team?"

"Fuck that. IV please, or I'll rip it out."

"I need gauze." I left and called Cheng on my cell phone. "The chole is leaving AMA. Refuses to see Vrac."

He sighed. "I'll come down."

"She may already be gone—"

He'd hung up on me. Good times. I grabbed some gauze. I could already hear her yelling at the nurses, "I'm leaving and you can't stop me. Vrac killed my aunt!"

She's not wrong, I thought as I hustled to her side. If more patients spoke up, the administration would stop covering up for him, $50,000 or no $50,000 donation.

Andrea pulled the tape off the IV.

"I said I'd rip it out with my teeth," the patient told me.

"I brought the AMA form."

"You know what you can do with the AMA form. You've got a legit killer on your staff. My cousin Leon's going to take care of him, you know what I mean?"

Andrea's hands stilled. "Is that a threat? We have a zero tolerance policy for violence."

"I'm not threatening you."

"Or Dr. Vrac?" Andrea asked, pulling the IV and applying pressure before taping the gauze.

The patient sighed. "Facts. I'm giving you facts on Vrac."

I showed her the AMA form.

The patient shoved her way out of the bed. "I'm calling Leon."

48

MAY 22, 21:30

HOPE

"What a night," said Tori when I called her on my call room landline to brainstorm my next step.

"What if they deny everything and *I* look like the loopy one?" I lowered my voice. You can hear other people through call room walls.

I wanted to pace, but the phone cord tethered me to a small area between the bed, bedside table, and wall. A few call rooms boast a desk, but not this one. The curtain hung crooked, allowing street lamp light to shine into the small room, highlighting the one wire hanger dangling in my makeshift "closet."

"You know the right thing to do. You can't stay silent," Tori said.

I paused. Brave Hope wouldn't. But what about Scared Hope, Intimidated Hope, I-just-want-to-pass-this-rotation Hope? All valid Hopes!

"You have to report him. If you don't, I will."

"You weren't *there.*" My heart kicked against my chest wall. I closed my eyes, willing it to slow down. Water dripped from the tap in my adjoining bathroom. Back in med school, when my classmates had taken THC gummies, one of them had ended up stoned on call and nearly expelled. After a huge investigation by the university, my classmates had blamed me as the snitch, even though I hadn't said anything. Whispers followed me, I didn't match to plastics, and had to reroute my whole medical career. Maybe I wouldn't have matched to plastics anyway, but it makes me gun shy now.

"He's too dangerous for anyone to hesitate," said Tori. "He deliberately killed a patient by preventing a proper code. I'll report this in the morning and trigger an investigation. If St. Joe's covers it up, I'll go to the university."

"Me too." Speaking the words aloud solidified them in my mind. I had to speak up this time. "I'll email the Chief of Surgery and Chief of Staff. No admin is around in the middle of the night, and the coroner should trigger a criminal investigation over a suspicious death." I sighed. "You sound ... determined. Did you figure anything else out?"

"Tucker's messaged me about Mireille. Her CT was clear."

"Oh, thank God." No brain bleed. I closed my eyes.

"She's remembering a bit more. A white BMW hit her. She saw the car's logo."

"Holy crap!"

"Tucker called the police." Tori paused. "I've been going over a few things from that parking lot myself."

"You mean Trent? And the ... " My throat locked up on the word *ghost.*

"Exactly. I finished my drawing."

My cell phone binged from the bedside table, where I'd plugged it to recharge it. Tori had texted me her sketch from lunchtime, which felt like a lifetime ago.

She'd drawn a man. A young man, judging from his narrow face and lanky body. He stared out from the page, chin jutting in the air as he stood beside a motorcycle, and something about his defiance twigged a memory that I couldn't quite grasp.

I focused on the motorcycle. "You should send this to people who know motorcycles. That would help date this."

"I did. Griffin figured that bike's from the 1960s, maybe even the 1950s."

I would've whistled in appreciation, but I never figured out how. "So this is a historical picture."

"It's possible that someone kept a bike in vintage shape, but road salt erodes everything on Canadian roads. We think it's much more likely a throwback from when bikes like that were more common."

I examined the face sketch, trying to imagine him in the '60s or '80s. Would ghost guy love the Beatles? "His hair is kind of long and turned under at the bangs and all the way around. It's not a bowl cut, more like a mushroom."

Tori gave a small laugh. "They call it a pageboy. I already looked it up. It was popular in the 1970s and '80s."

"Okay, that gives us a time period and would explain the motorcycle. He looks young. He'd want the latest haircut." I stared at the picture and thought, *How did you die? Why are you haunting Tori?*

My skin crawled, reliving that moment of possession, and I turned my cell phone off and closed my eyes. "I'm sorry. I can't handle the supernatural angle. Could you look into it?"

"I get it. It's a lot. Griffin and I will work on it." Her voice soothed me through the landline. "In other news, Tucker reached out to the local vehicle repair shops, even though it's after hours. He had a few ideas."

"Wait!" I unlocked my cell to text Tucker as I spoke to Tori. "Did he try one named Roy's?"

"I don't know. He didn't mention it."

"That was the very first thing Vrac said to me. 'Are you from Roy's Car Service?' What if he let it slip, and that's his actual repair place?" I scrunched up my face. "This entire time, Vrac's bragged about his cars and offered to take me and Delilah out in his Mercedes. If he hit Mireille with his white BMW, that's why he's yelling about a BIXI bike."

Tori paused. "One other—"

"'*Beam* me up, Scotty.' Mireille meant a Beamer, a BMW. Even that stupid 'Young Man Dead' song came from a *BMW* commercial. She was trying to tell us all along!" As a non-car person, I'd never put those clues together, but Mireille had tried. "Vrac yelled about his

BMW and ... something like metallic white. He needed a new paint job after he smushed her because she was at the Joan Finn case. I've got to tell Tucker!"

"Hope, about the g—"

"One minute, please!" I called Tucker on my cell. He didn't answer, and could have been in the middle of a delivery, so I left a convoluted message that boiled down to *you have to try Roy's Car Service!*

Wait a minute. I could try them myself. Online, I found an automotive place run by Roy only a few blocks away, Garage Roy Mécanique et Entretien.

It wouldn't take much time to hit Mireille, then leave his car at Roy's. He could have walked to St. Joe's afterward with plenty of time to make his first case.

"Do you want to call me back later?" Tori asked, as my pager rang and vibrated, making me jump.

"No, but I'll have to let you go. Could you call Garage Roy?" I recited the number for her.

49

JANUARY 25, 18:50

GORDON

If Vrac had fiddled with the brakes on Charlie's car, Gordon could never prove it now. Jim reported that both Charlie and Nadia's bodies had been cremated and their car had been scrapped. Vrac would never breathe a word to incriminate himself.

Gordon tried to imagine how Vrac had felt. Even if he hadn't cut the brake lines, Vrac had upset Charlie to the point where the man might have taken a corner too fast or braked too late, with fatal consequences.

One fact remained: in a single month, Vrac had lost his brother, his mother, and his stepfather. He would have died himself if he'd agreed to get in the car and go to church.

Did he lash out at everyone now out of survivor's guilt, or survivor's remorse?

Gordon remembered Ms. Cortese's description and shook his head. Vrac's drive for perfectionism had pre-dated that horrible month. Even so, Gordon had uncovered the biggest piece of the puzzle in Saskatchewan. The one that made Vrac run away from his adopted town.

Slowly, Gordon made a few more notes. Where did Vrac obtain the money to study medicine in the Caribbean? That was even more expensive than in Canada, although tuition wouldn't have been as egregious forty years ago.

Yes, Vrac had been the sole survivor of four. Did he receive some sort of insurance payout?

The residency in the U.S. would have cost him as well. Residents got paid less than minimum wage, and his cost of living would have at least doubled compared to the Caribbean. Gordon suspected that by the time Vrac returned to Canada, he would've needed to fill his coffers.

Enough to operate on crashing patients beyond his skillset?

Enough that he was willing to risk lawsuits, as long as his scalpel kept moving?

Probably not, but Gordon took photos of his paper notes and uploaded them to the cloud. He carefully tucked those notes inside a sheaf of anesthesia notes and research papers before locking his desk. Then he pressed the button for Jim's number, damn the cost.

Jim picked up right away. "What's up?"

"I ap-preciate everything you've done. I know you worked hard. The problem is—" Gordon swallowed. "It's all hearsay."

Jim's chair creaked before he answered. "I followed your lead. I did what you asked."

"Yeah, and I appreciate it, but I can't take this to court."

Jim snorted. "Who's asking you to?"

"I was hoping for something more c-concrete."

"We all hope for something."

Jim didn't care. Gordon wondered if he'd been set up by the principal and Jim and if they'd fed him a bunch of horse crap, but he'd searched for and found the three obituaries himself, now that he'd known which names to search.

"You gotta think outside the box. Between you and me, the best thing about being a private detective is that we're not hamstrung the way cops are. We don't have to follow all the rules and carry around crappy guns that make the bad guys laugh when we throw them back on the street. We can bend the rules a bit sometimes."

Gordon got the feeling that Jim was trying to tell him something. He stopped picking at his cuticles. "You want me to think outside the box."

"Exactly. I gave you good information. It's up to you to decide what you're going to do about it."

"Thanks." Gordon couldn't think. He needed to study for his exams. He needed to impress his preceptors. He needed to figure out what to do with the history of Vladimir/Waldo/Vadim Vrac.

Gordon decided to avoid it all by watching the video footage from the fridge.

If he caught Dr. Vrac tampering with Dr. Burns's lunch box, maybe he could bypass this messy history and find something current.

50

MAY 22, 22:45

HOPE

My phone rang after I finished orders on a patient with a small bowel obstruction. I answered it on my way back from the floor to my call room. "What's up, Tori?"

"I found Roy's," she said, in a hushed voice.

"You mean on the map?"

"No. I mean I'm here."

"Wait. It's the middle of the night. Is that safe?" My stomach clenched. "Did he admit to knowing Vrac?"

"Not yet."

"Is Griffin with you?"

"He's waiting outside."

"What!"

"Griff knows I'm inside. He'll grab someone if he has to. You're my second backup. I texted Tucker too."

"Tori, that's insane! How is he even open at 11 pm?"

"It's a one man show. I think he tinkers with cars all the time. We took a chance and came over. Griffin really does like old bikes."

"Even if Roy was there, why'd he let you in at this time of night?"

"I told him I was Vrac's resident, sent to check on his car."

It wouldn't have occurred to me to lie like that.

"Griffin came up with it, and I knew that if he checked, they'd mix up you and me anyway. Gotta go."

"Tori!"

"You can track me," she said, before she cut the call.

"Tori!" I yelled into the dead phone before I switched over to WhatsApp's tracking feature. I found her little dot with Griffin's dot almost superimposed. Tucker was in-hospital, like me, as expected.

But I was on call. How could I track Tori and make sure she was all right and still survive general surgery call with Dr. Vrac? Griffin was cool, but could he take on Roy and drag Tori away single-handed?

Good excuse to call Tucker. He picked up right away. No time to feel awkward. "Babe, you know that Tori's at Roy's Garage?"

"Yeah, with Griffin."

He'd read his texts, at least. "But she's alone inside the garage. Who knows what could happen?"

He exhaled. "I know you're worried, but Tori's a big girl. You have any other suggestions?"

"Another person standing guard," I said immediately. "Mireille's out. How about Anu?"

"Anu?" I could hear Tucker tapping his phone, looking for her number. "Okay, I'll text her. She lives pretty close. Maybe she won't mind going out at night."

"Good point. You know anyone else who might feel safer playing backup?"

"Sébastien."

If he wasn't still mad about the chest tube. I sighed. "Please try them. I'd never forgive myself if anything happened to Tori."

"Seb's already asking me what's going on. You don't seriously think that Roy will hurt Tori, do you?"

"Nothing's ever completely off the table, but I'm covering our bets."

"How do you think Roy's involved?"

"I think he's been covering up for Vrac, but I don't know how, how to prove it, or how to stop him."

"I've got some ideas," said Tucker. "You want to catch a crook, think like a crook."

That made me smile. "I'll do my best."

Tori started sending pictures to both of us.

"What is this?" I had to expand the photos and squint at them.

"Holy sh—oot," said Tucker.

"What?"

"She found evidence that he's been ordering parts, I assume for Vrac, because he wrote VV beside them all."

"So? Isn't that his job?"

"She couldn't find any receipts made out to the name Vrac. I bet he's been doing the work under the table."

"Damn it. She shouldn't be going through his books when he's right there."

Tucker ignored me. "Looks like Vrac pays cash but makes him redo things so much, he actually loses money every time."

I made a face. Yes, that sounded like Vrac. Make bank, make a big deal out of giving money away to the hospital foundations, but short-change the guy actually doing the work.

"I feel like I've seen the name Solomon Roy before too." Tucker snapped his fingers. "I saw him when I did surgery clinic with Dr. Vrac. He's a patient!"

"A patient?"

"Yeah from an MVC years ago. I can't remember all the details about the collision. Pelvic fracture, tib-fib, femur, ribs"—Tucker named all the fractures—"but he also had a tear to his small bowel. He was on so many narcotics, I asked Dr. Vrac if I should start tapering and move to Suboxone to manage his addiction."

"And?" I held my breath.

"Vrac cursed me out and took over the chart himself. Threatened to fail me because I didn't understand general surgery. But now that I know he's in Vrac's back pocket ... "

I hissed out my breath from between my teeth. "Vrac kept him hooked on narcotics on purpose!"

"While he worked on Vrac's cars off the books." Tucker whistled. "Kind of genius."

I sighed between my teeth.

"Evil genius, obviously," Tucker said.

"We need to prove all this," I said. "He's not going to give up much more. I don't want Tori in there by herself too long."

"Griffin says he can see her through the window because they have the shop lights on. Hmm."

"What?"

"Griff thinks that Roy let her in because he couldn't resist a pretty face. I don't like the sound of that."

"Me neither."

"I'd pop over myself if I could. But I've got a woman at 8 cm."

He meant a woman in active labour who would have to wait for 10 cm cervical dilation to push. "Primip?" That would mean a first time birth with a longer labor time.

"Multip." Already given birth before, which meant the baby could pop out anytime.

"No, you can't go anywhere," I agreed. "I want to, but Vrac would kill me, we've got consults up the wazoo, and I could get called to the next OR any second."

"For the gastric volvulus?"

"Yeah. The endoscopy didn't work. I don't want Vrac to kill her too."

"About that," said Tucker.

"Yeah?"

"Why do you think he killed the other guy?"

I stayed silent for a minute. "I have a theory."

"That you don't want to share?"

"I'm waiting for information. I need to check my e-mail, actually."

"I know when I'm not wanted."

I sighed. "You know that's not true."

He stayed silent for a minute. "Yeah."

My heart thumped. I waited for him to say something more. *Tell me, tell me. I love you. We can do this.*

Tori had said to let him come back to me on his own time, knowing that it might be never. Even so, I opened my mouth. "I'm totally—"

"On call. I get it. I'll call you later."

I swallowed loud enough that he could probably hear me. "Okay." My voice broke, which humiliated me. I blinked back tears.

"Hope." His voice shook too.

We stayed silent, reminding me of the early days with Ryan when neither of us wanted to hang up. *You hang up first. No, you.* Finally, we'd count to three and both hang up at the same time, because it was too hard to say goodbye.

Tucker and I did it a few times, too, so I said, "On the count of three."

"Uh huh." He didn't trust his voice, either.

I whispered, "Ee, ar, san," counting in Mandarin.

He choked back a laugh, and we both hung up, longing for more.

51

JANUARY 26, 00:13

GORDON

Gordon nearly fell asleep watching the video. Grainy, boring video that wouldn't be admissible in court, since he hadn't gotten permission from anyone to plant the camera in the first place. Heck, maybe they'd arrest him if they found it. What had made Gordon think that anyone had poisoned Dr. Burns's lunch? Or that they'd keep doing it?

Gordon's eyes slid shut. He dragged them open and jerked awake.

Onscreen, a hand reached for Dr. Burns's yellow lunch bag and opened it. A hand that didn't belong to Dr. Burns.

Gordon held his breath as the camera managed to capture the face that went along with it.

Gordon nearly stopped there.

I can't do this.

His phone rang, but he didn't recognize the number and didn't answer. He picked up the message afterward, expecting spam. Instead, a man's hourse voice reached his car. "Hello, my name is Leon. I need to talk to you. My mother was Joan Finn. I know you were in that operating room, and I wanted to ask you—"

Gordon hung up, hands shaking, his breath rasping in his throat.

Gordon was a doctor. He put people to sleep. What made him think he should start investigating Vlad Vrac, or that any good would come of it?

Now he had video evidence he didn't dare show the police, and Joan Finn's son had called his personal number.

52

MAY 23, 00:28

HOPE

I stared at my pager, willing it to go off and call me to the OR to help Ms. Wells. That would also distract me from angsting about Tori, who'd fallen ominously silent.

Griffin? Everything okay? I wrote.

Nada. I couldn't call either of them in case it set off Roy's alarm bells. Even the ding of this text might rile him.

Can you go check on Tori? I messaged Tucker, but he'd stopped answering too. Probably delivering a baby.

I brought up the map of Roy's. Google estimated it as an 11 minute walk each way, or a four minute drive.

Did I dare leave the hospital property to check on her? On call, I never left the building, especially with an OR case pending. On the other hand, tonight could not get any worse. The big kahuna planned to fail me and I'd alienated both seniors. Therefore ...

I slipped on my shoes, locked my call room door, and set off down the stairs. My pager would work outside the building. I aimed for Roy's garage. I breathed in the cool night air, heard the crickets chirp, and could not regret my decision. Outside, I might catch Tori's scream, or hear Griffin shouting for help, without the cold walls of the hospital muffling them.

I hesitated before exiting the main doors.

If you're going to do this now, Hope, do it fast.

I took a deep breath and stepped on the mat to open the automatic doors.

Nothing. The doors stayed sealed. I belatedly remembered that they locked the main doors after hours. You had to go in and out through the ER. They only unlocked the main doors at nursing shift change, which was not now. This didn't usually affect me since I stayed locked inside all night on call, kind of like Rapunzel, only without the legendary hair.

I pivoted to my right, down the hallway to the ER, and nodded at the admitted patients on gurneys lined up to the vending machine. I couldn't help get them upstairs to a bed, but I could acknowledge their humanity. The same thing I do for unhoused people, sorry to say.

The double cast woman nodded back at me.

"Can you get me a drink, doll?" asked a skinny but spry-looking old man.

I gave him a sad smile. No alcohol here, and even water would be verboten if he needed surgery. "I wish."

He reached for my hand. I pulled away first but held out my index finger and thumb out in a gun hand at him, which made him chortle with glee.

An elderly woman stared at me, flushed, with unfocused eyes, and I made a mental note of her "bed number" (the paper taped to the wall above her head) to make sure someone kept an eye on her.

"Get me out of here," said a white-haired woman, shaking her IV pole at me.

"Your team will get you out as soon as possible, ma'am." I regretted not taking another hallway. More steps for me, but I hadn't expected so many admitted patients to talk to me.

My pager beeped, startling all of them except the septic-looking woman, and I cut into the ER by the side door to answer it. When I reached for the closest phone on the acute side, a nurse picked it up first, so I headed for the ambulatory section's phones.

Meanwhile, Tori messaged me and Tucker a picture of the outside of Roy's garage.

Tori got out. I exhaled and collapsed into an empty chair. The chair height deflated under my weight, but I didn't care. Tori had made it.

We good, Griffin added.

I sent them all a thumbs up and answered my page. Time for my OR. I called Tori while treating myself to a solo elevator ride up. "Thank you and you scared me. What happened?"

"I think he'll talk to me."

"The fact that he let you in there at midnight—"

"Yeah. It's a precursor. He'll talk." After a minute, she said, "The motorcyclist came."

"To Roy's garage?" I could believe in spectral appearances at garages at 1 a.m. "What did it say?"

Tori's footsteps slapped the sidewalk in time with Griffin's. "No words, but I could feel its presence. Much stronger inside the shop, and especially near the front bumper of Vrac's BMW."

I sucked in my breath. "Roy confirmed it was Vrac's?"

"No, he wouldn't confirm a lot verbally. But I saw the white BMW's paint scrapes and dents. I'll send you the two pics in a second. They're uploaded to the cloud already."

I squeezed my eyes closed. "We should share them with Mireille." Maybe not admissible in court, but I bet it would trigger a memory.

"I'll do it."

"She's supposed to rest her eyes for at least 24 hours with a concussion," I said. "So nothing until at least 5:45 am."

"She can talk on the phone. I'll leave her a voice mail in case she can't sleep."

My elevator binged. "You are the queen of investigations. And of the paranormal."

That made her laugh. "I don't know. You set a pretty high bar yourself."

The elevator doors labored their way open for me. I whispered, "I almost passed out in the parking lot. Doesn't get any lower than that. You take care of yourselves, okay?"

"Ten four," she said, which the nurses say at the end of answering an ambulance page.

No one lingered in the hallway outside OR 3. I quietly made a spiral Reiki sign that my med school friend Ginger had once shown me. I didn't necessarily believe in Reiki, but I needed to ward off evil before I stepped into the lair.

This time, I'd stay out of Vrac's reach.

This time, I'd stay silent unless someone explicitly asked me a question.

This time, I wouldn't make the mistake of scrubbing in unless the Grand Poobah expressly invited me. And maybe if I acted perfectly, he'd forget about failing me.

To my shock, when I pushed open the door, Ms. Wells met my eyes.

"Hello!" I quickly checked her vitals: 110/60, 108, 28, 94%. Not great, but in better shape than Trent.

Dr. Nanut frowned at me. "I'm glad you're here. She didn't want to go under before talking to you."

I didn't bother asking why. I reached up to take Ms. Wells's hand. "How can I help?"

"Help," she breathed.

It was the first word she'd spoken to me. "I'll try."

She frowned and gathered her strength. Even breathing took an effort, let alone forming words. "Get. That." She took one last breath. "Man."

Dr. Vrac, I assumed. Did she mean she'd help me put him away?

"Thank you," I said, pressing her hand.

"That all?" said anesthesia, clearly not impressed. "All done now?"

I waited, but Ms. Wells closed her eyes and lay back on the OR table, clearly exhausted. "I think so," I said.

"Good." Dr. Nanut quickly administered her drugs, and Ms. Wells's entire body relaxed into unconsciousness. I felt sad for Ms.

Wells, knowing how much pain she'd suffered, and how she'd hung on for even a few minutes to try and communicate—what?

Help. Get that man. I rolled the words in my head, shrugged, and filed them away for now.

"Let's get this party on the road." Dr. Vrac swung the door open and glared at me. "Where are the men?"

I blinked back at him and glanced around. No Singh. No Cheng. "I don't know."

"Well, you're not going to assist me when I've got a surgical R5 and R2! Go find them."

Jesus. Kicked out of the OR again.

"Will you be able to start the case without them?" asked Dr. Nanut.

"'Course I can. I can do everything! I'm a one man show. You should see my Audi!" he blustered.

I headed to the door, hiding my own doubts. Dr. Vrac was older than a lot of general surgeons. He complained mightily about Singh, but when Vrac changed hospitals, he forced McGill to transfer his right hand man to St. Joe's along with him, or even before him.

What if Dr. Vrac didn't know how to operate without the help of his chief resident?

I hustled straight out of the OR, not pausing at the dictation room within Vrac's earshot. From OR 1, I called locating and got the same confused security guard doubling as the operator after hours.

"I need the chief general surgery resident on call. The chief surgery resident, to this extension, 4917. Thank you." Better start with Singh, within spitting distance of graduation, not Cheng. I hung up and willed Singh to answer.

Instead, my pager beeped immediately, showing extension 4917.

I called locating back. "You called me, the general surgery R1, Dr. Hope Sze. I want the chief general surgery resident on call, Dr. Raj Singh. Ask him to call 4917."

"You want Dr. Zee?"

"No, I want Dr. *Singh,* the general. Surgery. Chief. Resident on call, paged to 4917."

Long silence. "I should call Dr. Vrac, the general surgeon on call?"

"No! I want Dr. *Raj Singh*. Raj Singh. Is he on your list?"

"I don't think so."

"S-i-n-g-h."

"I don't have anyone by that name."

"Normally, he'd do call at University College Hospital."

The guard sounded relieved. "Oh, you have to call University College Hospital."

"No! Dr. Singh's on call for St. Joe's right now. I just meant that if you have the UC list, you can try his cell phone."

"What?"

I sighed deeply and texted Cheng while I kept trying to make myself understood. "Do you see Dr. Raj Singh listed anywhere?"

"No."

"The chief resident or senior resident on call for general surgery?"

I heard papers rustling. "There's a senior resident?"

Good God. I checked my cell phone, but Cheng hadn't answered my text yet. "How about Dr. Mike Cheng?"

"Mike. Cheng." He flipped through some more papers.

"Michael Cheng. The general surgery junior resident."

My pager went off again to extension 4917. I silenced it. "No, you just called *me* again. Never mind. Goodbye." I hung up on "locating" and called the ER.

Andrea, one of my other favourite nurses, answered immediately. "St. Joseph's Emergency Department, how can I help you?"

"Andrea, we need Dr. Raj Singh. Did he come to get his nose fixed?"

"The gen surg senior?" She sounded surprised. "I haven't seen him."

"The chief. Dr. Vrac punched him during the OR. Sounded like he broke his nose."

"He punched his chief resident?"

"Yes. In OR 3. Dr. Singh was going to come get his nose fixed in the ER."

Roxanne took over the phone. "Hope, Raj never came down."

"Really?"

"Never saw hide or hair of him. Did Vrac really break his nose?"

"I heard his bones break, and it bled like stink." I didn't hold back. The more people who knew, the harder for Vrac to cover it up later.

"He should talk to the police. This is fucking ridiculous," said Roxanne.

"I want to, but Singh said no. He's not at the OR for Ms. Wells, and Vrac doesn't know what to do without him."

"Andrea and I have been here all night. We haven't seen Raj since you brought Trent up to the OR."

"Affirmative," I heard Andrea say.

"I'll check around," Roxanne continued, "but as far as I know, Raj never darkened our door again."

"Then where did he go?" I asked, almost to myself, before I hung up.

I called locating back. "Can you go through your call room records? Do you have a room for Dr. Raj Singh?"

"I told you, I don't know who that doctor is."

And yet he's been running your general surgery ward and OR for two months. "Could you please check the call room records?" I asked, striving for patience. They kept call room records separate from the doctor on call records. I'd seen the guards scrawl call room names down on a piece of paper.

"Just a minute." He plodded along. I could practically imagine him licking his finger and running his fingertip along the paper. "Hey, what do you know. This looks like Raj Singh."

"In what room number?"

"Aw, geez, I don't know if I should tell you."

"What's your name?"

"Henry."

"Henry, Dr. Singh is scheduled to operate with Dr. Vrac right now. Dr. Vrac can't operate without him. Do you know who Dr. Vrac is?"

"Yes." His breath puffed out in fear.

"Dr. Vrac gets angry when you cross him. Have you noticed?"

"Yes."

"Now, I can hang up and make Dr. Vrac come tell you he needs Dr. Singh. But he'll want to know your last name, Henry, and he'll hold a grudge against you personally. You're delaying this life-saving operation. We only operate in the middle of the night if someone's dying."

"It's room 6668!"

"Thank you, Henry." I hung up, not worried that he'd complain about me. He'd forget my name within a minute.

Then I beat it up to room 6668. The one next to mine.

53

JANUARY 29, 08:00

GORDON

"Leon Finn here again. I got your number through locating. We should talk about what happened to my mother one-on-one. Forget this lawyer stuff."

Gordon cut the voice mail. He'd set his phone on fire if his job didn't tether him to calls and constant updates.

His phone rang again. He shut his eyes, plugged his ears and hummed. "Shut up, shut up, shut up."

54

MAY 23, 01:12

HOPE

I rattled the call room's locked doorknob. "Singh! It's Hope Sze!"

Should have thought that one through. Even if Singh was holed up in his call room, I couldn't dissolve between the atoms of wood in order to grab him.

I banged on the door. "Singh. Singh, can you hear me?"

No answer from within, but someone else down the hall yelled, "Trying to sleep!"

"Sorry. It's an emergency."

"So's my sleep," he grumped. It sounded a bit like that med student, Greg.

I hated waking up hard-working residents and med students grabbing a few precious Z's, but Dr. Vrac's furious face crowded in my mind, and I kept banging. "We need you for the A case. Vrac doesn't know what to do. I'm sorry he hit you. That was horrible. I feel terrible about it, and I will talk to the police. I have at least one friend on the force who might be able to keep it quiet. Plus the university."

I flinched when a door cracked open down the hall to my left, but Tucker's pale face peered at me. "Hope, why are you waking everyone up?"

"I need Singh. We can't operate without him."

"Page him."

"I can't. Locating is stupid."

Tucker tipped his head in acknowledgement. "You don't have his cell number?"

"No, he didn't give it to me this morning. After Dr. Burns ... " None of us thought straight, basically.

Tucker nodded again. "And you're sure he's in here?"

"No. But he never made it to the ER after Vrac broke his nose, punching his face in front of the whole OR. I have a bad feeling about this."

"You have a bad feeling about everything." Tucker sent me a sideways smile.

"Justifiably!"

"I was just going to say. Justifiably." He banged on the door himself one more time before he pulled a tool out of his pocket. "Luckily, these locks aren't hard to jimmy."

My eyes widened.

"Hey, if you don't reserve your room in time, the guards will tell you there are none. Then you have to sleep on the couch in the residents' room and risk monkeypox."

I shuddered. This was a clear and present danger. Tucker advised me right from July first that sleep-deprived residents and medical students forgot to turn in their key (or maybe they're assholes who deliberately kept their key) at the end of their call. Then the guards checked their paper list, said that room was still full, and wouldn't release it for the next person. Which means they don't have enough call rooms for everyone on call. Thus I always reserve my call room early.

But if you were Tucker, you maintained a backup plan: pick the lock.

First, he locked his own call room door. "I've still got Mireille's bike."

"The police didn't want it?"

"They'll accept it in the morning. They found the story at least 'worth listening to.' Don't worry, I took photos and a video documenting everything, in case her bike goes AWOL. Already in the cloud, with sharing permissions for you and Mireille and Tori and Griffin."

I nodded. Montreal police shouldn't be so corrupt that Dr. Vrac could bribe his way out of a hit and run with a resident cyclist.

On the other hand, if Vrac tossed another $50,000 at police services, maybe he *could* bribe his way out.

Tucker kept jiggling the lock with what looked like a metal pin. He switched pins. "This doesn't work for every lock, but St. Joe's has these old-fashioned tumblers ... "

I started singing "Old Fashioned" by Panic! At the Disco.

Tucker joined in softly. I'm sure whoever was trying to sleep wanted to kill us, and yet I didn't care. Tucker had avoided me since calling off our engagement. Singing outside the call room felt like coming home.

"Shut up," a woman said.

I suppressed a laugh. Tucker whispered, "Sorry," before he clunked a tumbler in the door.

"The moment of truth," said Tucker, and swung open Singh's door.

The smell of blood hit us first.

55

FEBRUARY 2, 07:48

GORDON

Gordon got matched to Dr. Qadir, a neuro-anesthesiologist who didn't often work with first year residents.

Gordon tried not to look at Dr. Q's belly, obvious under her scrubs.

"It's okay, I'm surprised how huge I am too," Dr. Qadir said, not flinching as she drew up Fentanyl with practiced fingers. "I wear compression stockings, but otherwise, no big deal."

"Who'll cover for you during your mat leave, though?" asked Cindy, a nurse with prominent smile lines who often ran marathons.

"They've recruited a fellow from Qatar. I like to say that we're replacing Dr. Q with another doctor from Avenue Q."

"I got the pregnant one?" Dr. Vrac roared as he shoved his way into the room, and Gordon's teeth clenched.

Dr. Vrac barrelled toward Dr. Q. "Aren't you neuro? Why're you doing gen surg today?"

"I'm covering for Dr. Mangino," she said.

Dr. Vrac rolled his eyes. "Did she have nanny trouble again? God! Women and their 'child care issues.' If you want to be a doctor, be a doctor! Don't futz around with screaming babies. You'll end up with screwed up kids and a career in the toilet. Pick one."

"Spoken like a man who's never had to deal with child care," Dr. Qadir said evenly, her tone implying that no one would procreate with him. "Have you ever had an issue with my medical competence?"

Dr. Vrac sniffed. "I never work with you. You're wasting your time on shunts and 16-hour spine cases."

"You'll work with me today. How lucky for both of us." Dr. Qadir eyeballed him until Dr. Vrac turned to yell at Singh about a patient on the floor.

Gordon exhaled unevenly. Dr. Q said nothing, but the look in her eyes spoke volumes as she quickly checked the patient's vitals. Vrac didn't intimidate her, and she wouldn't put up with any of his shit. That felt good.

"A fair amount of anaesthesiology is handling other personalities," she said, replugging a wire without bothering to lower her voice.

A young circulating nurse, Rebecca, changed the subject. "Do you know if you're having a boy or a girl?"

"All boy," said Dr. Q, patting her enormous abdomen. Gordon didn't know where to look, so he checked the monitor himself.

"Did you name him already?" Rebecca continued.

"Michael," said Dr. Q. "It's my father's middle name too."

"Oh, that's beautiful," Rebecca clasped her hands together. "I have a cousin named Mike."

Dr. Q nodded. "We'll call him Michael, but I know most people will call him Mike or Mikey."

"Or Mikhail?" Gordon put in.

Dr. Vrac's shoulders tightened under his scrubs. Gordon pretended not to notice as he raised his voice. "That's the Russian variation. You may have heard of Mikhail Gorbachev."

"Oh, and the ballet dancer, what's his name?" asked one of the nurses as she adjusted the drape.

"Mikhail Baryshnikov," said Dr. Q. "Yes, we researched the name Michael. It's originally a Hebrew name derived from the question mī kā'ēl, which means 'who is like the Lord?'"

Gordon kept his eyes averted from Dr. Vrac, whose brother was "with the Lord" now, if you believed in the afterlife.

Rebecca scrunched up her nose. "It's a name from the Bible, right?"

Dr. Q nodded and permitted a smile to cross her face as she adjusted the patient's position. "Michael is the archangel who leads the war against Satan, guiding the other angels to victory."

A war against Satan! Gordon suppressed a laugh. He wouldn't pretend that Vrac was Satan.

On the other hand, Vrac was the most Satanic surgeon Gordon had ever met, bar none.

"Michael and Gabriel are the only two archangels recognized by Muslims, Jews, and Christians alike," said Dr. Q, signalling that the patient was ready for surgery now. "Let us begin."

Dr. Vrac stepped forward. For once, he hadn't yelled or blustered.

"Well? Get on with it," he told Singh, who looked vaguely surprised at the lack of animosity.

Mikhail, *thought Gordon. The key to Vrac's humanity lies in Mikhail. What do I do with this?*

56

HOPE

"No," I said.

"I'm calling a code!" Tucker yelled.

I advanced into the bathroom. Tucker threw on the lights.

Singh lay crumpled in the bloody shower stall, eyes staring, a scalpel fallen near his right hand.

I didn't have any gloves, but I waded into the blood, kicked the scalpel toward the toilet, and threw myself on Singh, checking for a breath, a heart beat, before I started CPR.

"No no no no no no no no no," I said with every indentation of his chest.

Singh's eyes never blinked.

57

FEBRUARY 9, 08:35

GORDON

"Leon Finn. But you probably knew that. I guess you're not going to call me. I've got to say, I'm disappointed. My lawyer told me not to call you, but I wanted to give it a try. I got some things I want to say, and I bet you do, too."

Gordon paused the voice mail. The CMPA had told him not to call Leon Finn, saying, "It's best to go through the system and ensure clear communication. If you really want to communicate with him, you can write a letter and have your advisor read it first."

Everything was screened. Everything was passed through lawyers. In a way, Gordon admired Leon for cutting through red tape. But Gordon didn't dare answer, even though he forced himself to press play again.

"If you won't talk, I'll go back to the lawyers," said Leon Finn's recorded voice. "You know I will."

58

HOPE

I do remember Tucker pulling me off of Singh. "You have to let go, Hope! You have to let them in!"

"You got a pulse?" I yelled back at him.

Tucker pointed at the bilateral wounds in Singh's neck and the blood in both inguinal areas instead of answering.

"You feel anything?" I insisted, but I let a woman in gloves shoulder me aside to take over CPR.

"We need blood!" I told them. Litres and litres of blood. Talk about a massive transfusion protocol.

"Come with me," said an older and authoritative Black nurse whose badge read Denise. Although she didn't touch me, mindful of my Carrie-on-prom-night (buckets of blood) appearance, I followed her to a corner near the door, allowing the rest of the team into the bathroom to take over the code while Denise said, "Listen to me, darling, you need a shower."

"A shower," I repeated, examining the blood spatter on my own hands.

"That's right, if the police don't need you right away." Denise nodded at the doorway.

"The police?" I repeated, and peered at the doorway. I spotted a man in uniform cutting through the crowd before my gaze locked on Dr. Vrac's panicked features. For once, Vrac stood at the back instead of forcing his way to the forefront.

"You motherfucker," I said.

Denise's mouth opened, but I'd already honed in on Vrac. Everyone automatically stepped back, trying to distance themselves from my bloodstained body. Even the two police officers momentarily shied away from me, allowing me to get right up in Vrac's face and tell him, "He didn't even use the bed."

Vrac's head jerked down to the bathroom floor, where the rest of the team tried to revive Singh.

"That's right," I told him. "He did it on the floor."

Raj Singh couldn't stand the constant torrent of racist abuse, but he couldn't report his corrupt supervising physician either. So Raj had slashed both his femoral arteries with a scalpel, a quick and easy way to die—if you don't have people pounding on the door. The problem with femoral arteries is that they're in your groin area, on either side of your crotch. Not how you want your junior resident to find you. Then Raj had switched to his carotids.

Throughout the entire ordeal, Raj hadn't wanted to contaminate the bed, which other residents would have to sleep on. So his last act had been to squeeze himself into the grimy St. Joseph's shower stall while he killed himself.

"I'll get your medical license taken away if it's the last thing I do," I told Vrac. "Criminal court, civil court, whatever it takes. You will never hurt another doctor or patient or nurse again."

Denise said, "You need some air, Dr. Sze."

"I need justice," I replied between my teeth.

"Let me help you with that." Denise coaxed me to the window, where the anemic curtain fluttered above the radiator and a small desk. Denise meant to keep me away from Dr. Vrac yet still within reach of the police, but my eyes locked on the letter neatly placed in the middle of the desk.

I swiped at the letter before I remembered my blood hands. "Tucker!"

He found me in two steps. "Hope—"

"I need that letter scanned and uploaded everywhere before you give it to the police. It may be the last thing Singh ever says."

To whom it may concern,

I, Raj Singh, want to make it clear what happened on September 14th, during the operation on Joan Finn.

A scrub-clad arm swooped down. "Give me that." Vrac's fingers started to close over the page.

I thrust my arms between him and Tucker. "Get away from him."

"Dr. Sneeze—"

"Don't call me that."

He made an exaggerated face. "Dr. Sze, if you'll insist on hysteria—"

I stared him straight in the eye. "Murderer."

Someone else gasped, and he recoiled. "What did you say?"

"You killed him." I gestured to the bathroom. Tucker had retreated to the hall with the letter and his phone. I needed to distract Vrac the way that a bird will mimic a broken wing to distract a predator from engulfing a nearby nestful of eggs. "You killed Raj Singh as surely as if you held the scalpel. You broke his nose, and you tried to break his spirit every day for five years. You sexually and verbally assaulted me. And what about Joan Finn?"

His entire face collapsed like a shrunken head. No more Mercedes for me. "You weren't there, you stupid chink bitch."

The crowd shifted with every insult. They murmured in protest. I caught the gleam of someone's phone camera out of the corner of my eye and nearly smiled. Instead of shrinking from his attack, I grew paradoxically taller. "I wasn't at Joan Finn's operation. But I did watch you kill Trent Jones, Joan's scrub nurse, tonight."

The rest of the crowd subsided into silence.

"Then Nikki e-mailed me her papers, including the lawsuit that named everyone involved: yourself, Dr. Burns, who lies in ICU tonight—"

"I didn't—"

"Raj. Singh." My stomach clenched. I had to grind past his name. "Trent Jones, the scrub nurse you hit with your second car and left to die in our parking lot before killing him on the OR table."

"How dare you. You have no proof. I'll get you on slander and libel charges."

"Several witnesses watched you stab Trent's spleen on the table," I told him. "I'm one of them."

Vrac lunged forward to slap me across the face. I sidestepped and caught his bare arm with my bloody hand. Most of Singh's blood had dried already, but enough remained to imprint his skin. Vrac recoiled.

"Now you have Singh's blood on you, literally," I said.

Vrac tried to wipe it off, spreading it to his other hand in a Lady Macbeth move.

I smiled horribly at him. "Trent came to St. Joe's to meet Mireille Laroque, the former medical student operating with you that day, who was also named in the lawsuit. You had already hit her and her bicycle with your white BMW. She made it, partly thanks to her helmet." Tori had texted me some crucial information. "Her helmet's GoPro camera will testify against you, too. She remembers her password now and can unlock the footage of you hitting her, already uploaded to the cloud in real time."

His throat spasmed. He loomed over me for an epic yell.

I spoke first, channelling every human being he'd silenced over the years. "You tried to kill everyone on that OR team, saving Singh for last because you needed his surgical skills."

Vrac jabbed his index finger in my face. "Shut up."

"No."

"Bitch, I'll string you up. You know who my lawyer is?"

"I don't care if you have *ten* lawyers. My colleagues and I will *bury* you."

"Blackmail too." His hands fisted. "You don't think I saved your emails? I've got someone tracing your IP. A private detective who does forensic computing. The best of the best."

"I don't know what you're talking about," I told him. "I never e-mailed you. My schedule was arranged by the university."

"You blackmailing bitch, I've got proof too!" He punched me in the stomach, walloping the wind out of me.

59

FEB 10, 22:55

GORDON

Gordon created a burner email address to write to Dr. Vrac.

I need to talk to you, *Gordon typed.*

He stopped there. No signature, nothing to identify him. It might get caught in a spam folder, but it wouldn't get traced back to his IP. Gordon pressed send.

No response. Gordon typed a new one and sent it the next night.

I know about Mikhail

WHO THE FUCK ARE YOU? *Vrac slammed back an hour later.*

Someone who knows

LEAVE ME ALONE, YOU MUTHERFCKER!

Gordon hesitated before the fourth message.

Nadia

WHO THE FUCK IS THIS? I'M HIRING SOMEONE TO COME AFTER YOU?! YOU CANT THREATEN ME LIKE THIS.

Gordon paused, but he couldn't stop now. He gave one more name.

Charlie

WHAT DO YOU WANT? YOU WANT MONEY?

Gordon didn't know whether to laugh or puke. No, he didn't want money.

Gordon remembered Joan Finn on the OR table. He remembered Dr. Burns's agonized face.

Gordon thought of losing his medical career.

Then he emailed Dr. Vrac again.

60

MAY 23, 02:25

HOPE

I keeled over, struggling to breathe.

Vrac continued to shout.

I couldn't process his words. I needed air, a terrifying feeling. I could see everyone and hear them, but when I tried to inflate and deflate my lungs, no air moved.

"You hurt Hope," Tucker said.

That, I heard clearly. I whirled to face Tucker, still unable to breathe, but my hands outstretched to stop my man.

Tucker's fist lashed forward, directly for Vrac's abdomen.

I tried to cry out, but still couldn't make a sound. My hands flailed in the air.

Cheng blocked the blow, turning Tucker aside.

I regained my air. For a second, all I could do was suck air. In. Out. In. Out.

Tucker launched himself at Vrac again.

"He's not worth it," said Cheng, holding him back.

Tucker broke free. A big orderly promptly pinned Tucker's arms behind his back.

"Tucker," I managed to whisper.

Tucker's head cranked toward me.

I love you, I mouthed at him.

His entire face and neck flushed while his eyes stuck to mine. He didn't say it back, but he didn't need to after trying to deck the world's meanest surgeon for me.

The police shouldered their way into the room, and the orderly slowly released Tucker.

One look in the bathroom, and the police radioed for more help.

"What happened here?" asked a clean-shaven young, white officer.

I pointed at Dr. Vrac. "This man has systematically abused his residents to the point where one of them committed suicide tonight. I would personally like to report him for physical and sexual assault."

"Yeah?" Vrac pushed his words out between clenched teeth. "I'd like to charge *you* with *blackmail."*

I shook my head. Before I could refute him, Tucker said, "I've already contacted Ronald Lapierre about this, but I have video evidence of a white BMW striking a resident on a bicycle this morning in front of St. Joseph's Hospital. The resident's name is Dr. Mireille Laroque."

The officer looked at his buddy, a slightly older Black man who radioed for backup.

"I'm a victim of blackmail," Vrac called as they led him to another room for questioning. "I can prove it! They said they would ruin me. They said they knew everything and that the investigation would bring it all to light. They said I had to confess. Well, I won't. You call my lawyer! The best, most expensive lawyer in the province. He'll drain the Montreal police budget by morning. I can't wait to see him destroy you."

61

MAY 23, 02:30 (REAL TIME)

APARTMENT

GORDON

Gordon's phone rang.

He'd silenced it because he wasn't on call, but he did allow repeated calls to ring through in case his parents or sister needed him.

He picked up his phone and squinted at the screen.

NO CALLER ID

He ignored it, but his heart hammered and his breath grew short.

Leon Finn had called him three times before finally giving up.

Had Leon Finn blocked his own caller ID and moved to harassing Gordon in the middle of the night?

Gordon stared at the ceiling, counting to 100, before he dared check his messages.

No new voice mail.

He closed his eyes and willed himself to sleep.

62

MAY 22, 02:50

HOPE

"Can you come to the station for a formal statement?" The Black officer, whose badge said Thompson, led me to a quiet corner of the main room. I still felt everyone's eyes on me, but at least we'd moved a few metres away.

The only one I wanted was Tucker, and the other officer had taken him.

"I wish I could, but I'm still on call." I checked my watch: almost 3 a.m. "There's no one else to cover me. We've just lost our senior resident and our attending. We have a woman on the OR table."

I checked on Cheng, who seemed to organize the rest of the staff into leaving the room. Who would take care of Ms. Wells now? He'd probably call another surgeon in, if someone answered the phone. My mind flashed to Dr. Pierce. *She's fierce.*

Officer Thompson sighed. "What time does your call finish?"

"Well, technically, 8 a.m., but I'd stay later if they need me. And they need me."

Thompson's chin dipped in acknowledgment before he flipped to a new page in a small, black spiral ring notebook, pen already in hand. "How do you spell your name?"

As I spelled out Hope Sze, a new officer, a stern-looking older white woman, entered the room. Tucker hailed her. My shoulders relaxed a little, especially when he pulled a camera out of his pocket.

Even if Vrac wormed out of punching Singh and egging him on to commit suicide.

Even if he managed to get away with grabbing my ass and punching me in the stomach.

Even if I couldn't prove he'd stabbed Dr. Burns with a needle.

Even if we couldn't prove he'd punctured Trent's spleen or killed Joan Finn, he should not get away with a filmed hit and run of Dr. Mireille Laroque.

Thompson's ballpoint pen poised above the paper, ready to transcribe. "What is your role in the hospital?"

"I'm a family medicine resident studying general surgery this month. My attending surgeon is—was—Dr. Vrac." I explained the roles of Dr. Singh and Dr. Cheng and spelled their names also.

They didn't need me in the operating room for Ms. Wells, I realized, with a pang. Even if the new surgeon felt sorry for me, they'd need me to run the ER consults and the wards so they could concentrate on saving her life.

"In your own words, what happened here tonight?" Thompson asked.

"I was looking for Dr. Singh. He's my senior resident." I began filling in the story, but realized I'd have to mention Tucker picking the lock. "We managed to get in the room," I ended up saying awkwardly.

Thompson's eyes narrowed. "How did you get into the room? Wasn't it locked?"

"Yesss." I knew I should speak normally, but my brain had stopped firing all its neurons.

"Did you have a key?"

"No. I did try my key." I patted my pockets and showed him my call room key.

Thompson looked unimpressed. "What's that?"

"The key to my call room."

He shook his head. "Your call room? Why did you think it would work on a different room?"

I shrugged. "At St. Joe's, anything is possible, including giving us all the same call room key."

"If you didn't have a key, how did you get in?"

"We figured out a way to get in by playing with the door knob." There. True yet sufficiently vague.

Thompson shook his head, but let it go. "Why did you think it was so important to enter the room, that you had to force your way in?"

"Dr. Singh hadn't come for the surgery. Dr. Vrac asked me to find him. I knew something was wrong," I realized aloud. No matter how dire the situation—and it didn't get any worse than Dr. Vrac—for a surgeon not to show up at the OR table? In the depths of my subconscious, I did worry that only death could keep him away.

Even from OR 3, my brain whispered.

"And what did you see when you opened the door?"

"I saw him lying on the floor of the shower stall in a pool of blood." I swallowed. I had pronounced dead bodies before, of course, usually elderly people who had lost a long battle with cancer. Sad but not shocking.

This one made me take a deep breath. Raj Singh had been one of the good guys, destroyed by the system as surely as a gladiator tossed in the ring in Ancient Rome. I envisioned Raj facing a lion, armed only with his brain and a scalpel.

"You recognized him immediately?"

"Yes, but he looked—" Ghastly. Pale. Blank. If Raj's parents descended upon us, sobbing, should I tell them he was at peace now? Would they believe me?

Maybe he did rest easier because his letter incriminated Dr. Vrac, testifying against Vrac on Joan Finn's behalf.

"Joan Finn," I said aloud.

Thompson stopped writing. "What does this mean?"

"I'm sorry, I got distracted. Dr. Singh named the case of the patient who died in the OR in September, while under the care of Dr. Vrac and others. May I check my phone?"

"No, we need to finish this first," said Thompson. "Describe what you saw."

Fair enough. My turn to wait, like when I told patients to hang on so I could finish a quick history and physical exam before they peed. Still, I couldn't concentrate as I mechanically answered his questions, trying not to flinch as I detailed the size of the pool of blood and how I'd dived in while Tucker called for help.

"How was he lying in the shower?" Thompson asked.

I blinked at him. "Head and neck and part of his back against the wall, the rest of him on the floor, his legs sticking out in the room, his body in the middle of the blood. You can see it for yourself."

"I need you to describe it for me."

I did my best to estimate distances and liters of blood while my 3 a.m. brain zoomed onto another topic.

Vrac had somehow jeopardized or outright killed many people at that fateful OR: Joan Finn herself, Dr. Burns, Mireille the then-medical student, Trent the scrub nurse, and now Singh the chief resident.

Even with my rudimentary OR experience, I knew more people had been present. What about the circulating nurse? I itched to check Nikki's email. Hadn't they named an anesthesia resident too?

"When did the others arrive in the room?" Thompson glanced at the blood drying on my hands and clothes, barely able to hide his disgust.

"Maybe within five to ten minutes?" My stomach roiled too. Under my nails, my cuticles, between my toes, even the skin of my neck and ears itched with drying blood. Singh had been exposed to blood borne pathogens every day of his working life. I have a horror of catching HIV or Hepatitis C. Both are treatable, but no one wants those. "Could I take a shower now?"

Thompson shook his head. "We're nearly finished. When do you think the other people arrived? Five minutes or ten?"

I tried to think. "Definitely within ten minutes. We're on the sixth floor, away from the patient floors. Night time, things are slower, and we never have codes on this floor. They might have thought it was a mistake." I squeezed my eyes shut. Horrible to think of any delay in

Raj Singh's care, but the logical part of my brain knew it hadn't made any difference.

He'd wanted to escape. He'd seen only one way out.

"Did you notice anything unusual about the behaviour of other people in the room?"

How to say that I'd been so shellshocked that I'd blanked out most of this code? The truth made it easy. "No, I didn't notice anything unusual." My mind had operated on empty for the past, ooh, three hours. Like the famous Far Side cartoon: Excuse me, sir, my brain is full. Even before we lost one of the good ones.

Thompson flipped his notebook pages, checking for things he'd missed, giving me a few minutes to think.

I itched to talk to Nikki.

Even if they didn't name the circulating nurse in the lawsuit, they wouldn't run an OR without one. Quite often, nurses would substitute for each other, so there could have been two scrub nurses and two circulating nurses who'd witnessed the case.

If I'd stumbled into a surgical "And Then There Were None" scenario, I couldn't rest without a detailed list of every individual in that OR and their whereabouts tonight. At minimum, I needed to warn them. As soon as possible.

63

MAY 23, 03:00

GORDON

Gordon's phone buzzed with a new message from a blocked number.

I know its you

Gordon covered his eyes. Spammers wouldn't contact him in the middle of the night.

come to st joes

"I'm not going anywhere," Gordon told the empty air. His phone buzzed again.

you want to know about mike?

ill tell u what u want 2 know

n

c

v even

ill tell u

Gordon translated this: Mike. Nadia. Charlie. Vrac. I'll tell you everything. Had Vrac finally cracked? Or did Leon Finn want to share something? But why now, in the middle of the night? Why at St. Joe's?

He shouldn't answer. He shouldn't go.

But after ten minutes of pacing, Gordon typed, Who is this?

His phone buzzed with an instant answer.
st joes OR 3
NOW

64

MAY 23, 03:21

HOPE

When Thompson finally let me walk out of Raj's room, my phone buzzed.

Nikki?

I exhaled but refused to touch it to answer it until after my shower. The dried blood contracted, pulling on my skin, and the itch drove me insane. I wanted to roll my eyes up and snarl at the staff who whispered and eyeballed me.

Get this off of me.

Now I understood why Lady Macbeth had gone mad. Guilt, shame, fury, but also the reek and the grotesque sensation and stench of dried blood.

I did check my pager, which had remained mercifully silent. At this rate, we'd end up killing off everyone in the hospital and they'd have no one left to page me about.

Then I locked the door of my call room, tossed my disgusting clothes in the sink, and launched myself into the shower as soon as the temperature reached lukewarm.

Shoot. I hadn't brought any soap, shampoo, or conditioner into the shower with me, but the water sluicing off my body had already turned dark red, so I scrubbed my body with my nails, keeping my eyes and mouth as firmly shut as possible so I didn't have to drink Singh's blood, too.

After I got the worst of it out, I cracked my eyes and found that someone had abandoned a piece of hospital soap on a ledge. Gross, but better than blood, so I compromised by rubbing the soap on my hands, then my hands on my face and body, as if that degree of separation would make any bloody difference.

I winced. I'd never use bloody as a swear word again in my life without catapulting back to this moment.

But the water washed away some of my fear and warmed me up again, along with another thought:

Tucker loves me. And he'll help me figure out this godawful mess.

In fact, that might have been who tried to call me. And if not, I'd text Nikki.

I nearly whistled to myself until I reached for the non-existent towel and realized the only thing I had to dry myself off with, as well as re-wear? Scrubs utterly drenched in blood.

65

MAY 23, 03:40

HOPE

Ex-fiancé time. I shook my hands to dry them a bit, applied some hand sanitizer, swiped the remnants over my phone, and dialled Tucker using the speakerphone.

"I got the strangest call," he said immediately.

"This one is stranger. Tucker, I need a favour."

"You know how I have friends at UC?"

"You have friends everywhere, which is awesome. I need new scrubs."

"Yeah, so this guy called me in the middle of the night. I don't think you'd know him. He's kind of shy, doesn't party much."

I raised my voice. *"Tucker.* I don't care about your old pals right now. I just washed the blood off myself."

"Oh?" That caught his attention.

"I'm dripping water on the floor. I need new, non-bloody scrubs and a towel."

"You need a towel," he repeated. His tone dropped as he pictured me naked, which made my nipples tighten, but now was not the time.

"I couldn't wait to wash the blood off, but I don't have any new scrubs. Or a towel."

"Yeah." He still sounded stunned.

"I'd call Tori, but she's at home sleeping. If you leave me a towel and some scrubs outside my door, I could grab them."

"Then you'd have to open your door naked," he said, still low.

"Well, open it a crack. I mean, enough to grab the stuff. But—"

"I can bring them right to you with a towel and a fresh set of scrubs. I even have clean socks. You want my clean underwear too?"

"Uh ... " Awfully intimate, but did I want to go commando if Dr. Vrac might reappear to squeeze my butt cheeks any minute? I cleared my throat. "Yeah. I guess that would be good."

"Will you unlock your door if I knock and say a secret word?"

My stomach clenched like Vrac had punched me again. It took me a second to retrieve the sexy. I failed, but I tried to sound normal. "Um. Yes?"

"How about ... " He whistled "Walk Like an Egyptian," which made me laugh.

"I can still twerk, too," he said softly.

"I bet you can."

"I've never been so scared as when he hit you," Tucker said. "I wanted to kill him."

"Me too."

"Let me grab my stuff and come to your call room."

For a booty call? Tucker had avoided me up 'til now, but maybe after Vrac ran down Mireille, punched Singh, and socked me, Tucker realized life was short and could no longer resist me?

"Right," I said unsteadily.

"See you soon, Hope."

"See you soon."

Minutes later, the knock sounded at my door. Bap bap-bap-bap-bap. BAP! BAP!

"What's the secret word?" I asked, feeling silly, but our call room doors don't have peepholes, and that didn't sound like "Walk Like an Egyptian," especially when I was naked and shivering.

The knocks came again. Bap bap-bap-bap-bap. BAP! BAP!

The rhythm sort of mimicked "Walk Like an Egyptian" with an extra beat on the end, but Trivial Pursuit Tucker had already taught me that this was a completely different song called "Shave and a Haircut, Two Bits."

Which made me think someone other than Tucker knocked on my door.

Bap bap-bap-bap-bap. BAP! BAP!

I texted Tucker. *Are you at the door already?*

Floor called. Give me a minute.

So who the fuck was outside my door, knocking and refusing to speak?

I called the security guard. "I need security."

"I'm security," said the same young voice as earlier.

"I need you to come to my call room. Someone is knocking and refusing to identify himself."

"What room?" He sounded half-asleep.

I told him. "And, uh, if you have a blanket and some spare clothes, I'd really appreciate it."

"You need clothes?"

"You heard about the other call room doctor?"

"Yeah!" Now he was wide awake. "I didn't get to go!"

"I attended his code and can't wear those scrubs anymore." *Sorry, Raj.* "Could you send a patient gown up to me? I'll take anything, but first I need you to get rid of whoever's at my door."

"I'm on it! I'll call Frank and ask him to bring you a gown too."

"Two gowns if you can." I'd prefer not to expose my rear end. This was a very bum-oriented day. Appropriate, because general surgery is all about rectal exams and diseased bowel. I repeated my call room number before I hung up.

66

MAY 23, 03:52

HOPE

The knocking stopped, maybe so the stranger could eavesdrop on me and Tucker.

"Who is it?" I called again.

No answer.

Had the stranger left?

My pager beep beep beep beeped.

Fuck.

I answered it. "Hello?"

"We need you in OR 3," said Cheng.

"For Ms. Wells?"

"Yes," he ground out, "but we're running another code first."

"What?"

"We shipped her back to her room during the last code—"

Singh. I squeezed my eyes shut.

"—and now there's some guy on the table."

My heart thudded. "Is he a resident wearing his ID badge?"

Cheng sounded amazed when he said, "Yeah. You're right. Gordon Cole."

I swore a few times. "I'm coming, but I need something to wear. I'm covered in Singh's blood."

"Shit. I'll get an orderly to send something up when we get a second."

A party converged on my call room. Better than alone time with whoever tried to con me into opening my door, as confirmed by Tucker's text: *Emergency delivery. I left the clothes by your door. Next time.* 😊

I exhaled. Good news: clothes lay right outside my door. Bad news: I must open the door to get them.

Should I risk donning my gore scrubs for the split second I opened the door? I'd want to shower again afterward, but the code meant I didn't have time.

I strode back and forth in front of the door, searching for a shadow that would confirm either a stranger lingering or the clothes awaiting me, but in all of broke ass St. Joseph's Hospital, only the call room door was built to last. It stretched almost to the carpet. Even with my phone light at the gap, I couldn't make out a telltale shadow.

Because the door was too secure, my light too dim, or because ... ?

"Hello?" I called softly.

No one answered.

Next I called Tori. Her number rang four times before clicking over to voice mail.

Should I try Griffin? I didn't know him as well. She'd only started dating him a few months ago.

Security guard—Frank would have to dig up a patient's gown and towel in the ER, make his way to the sixth floor, and find the correct room. Not rocket science, but time consuming.

Cheng's orderly—non-existent until the code ended or he could spare a hand.

I started to chew on a fingernail before I gagged and ran my mouth under some water to rinse it out, and washed my hands again too.

I had a few choices. I could sit here and wait despite the code. Civilians know to don their own oxygen mask before their children's when their airplane plunges toward the earth. Well, I could dress myself before a code.

I could call the police, but to say what? A person knocked on my door? Not a federal offence. I could tell them that someone was killing every individual from the Joan Finn case. Concerning, but how would that make them rush to my side to dress me?

Time to make a decision.

I hit the bathroom, holding my breath at the smell of blood. I reached into the pile of discarded scrubs and picked out the underwear and bra.

I couldn't open the door without a stitch on. I wanted to help with the code, of course (another code! Worse than a TV show!), but I'd distract more than help in my current state. What would Dr. Vrac say or do if I ventured out in my underthings?

This was a record number of codes in 24 hours. Seriously, a small hospital doesn't get this many.

Maybe at UC. Which made me think of Gordon Cole. I checked my phone. Yes, they named Gordon Cole in the lawsuit. The only physician not working at St. Joe's and the only one who'd escaped up until now. He worked at UC and should have known to stay away from Vrac's new hospital.

How did Gordon end up in OR 3 in the middle of the night?How did they lure him here?

In the meantime, I wanted Tucker's clothes. How could I arm myself? I eyed the call room. Although it didn't include a desk, it did boast a metal railing that acted as a primitive closet next to the bathroom. A solitary wire coat hanger hung on it, waiting for me.

I tiptoed to the door, shivering, and worked the wire between the door and the carpet. It ran into something soft mid-door. Tucker's clothes had made it. I exhaled and pressed my ear against the door.

No one coughed or spoke, and Tucker hadn't mentioned seeing anyone when he dropped off the clothes. The intruder should have left.

Paranoid, but better paranoid and alive than dead and reckless. I called Nikki despite the zero percent chance she'd pick up at this hour, especially since I'd hidden my caller ID. "Hi."

She answered right away. "Hope Sze, right?"

"Yes!"

"Good. I need your help."

"I need yours first. Can you come up to my call room? I have no clothes. Long story."

"Vrac?" she asked.

"Indirectly. I'm afraid to open the door. Someone knocked on it, and Vrac already grabbed me and wants to tutor me."

"Join the club," she said, which made my heart twinge. "I'll be there. Which call room?"

I told her and asked, "Are you in the unit?" The ICU.

"No, I'm at home, but I'm a pro at getting to the hospital in record time. Give me 15 minutes."

I chewed my bottom lip. "Okay."

"I know that's a dog's age in medicine, but you have to trust me. Don't open that door."

"Even if Cheng calls me again for the code?"

"Another code?" Her voice sharpened.

"Yes."

"For someone connected to the Joan Finn case?"

"I'm not supposed to say, but—" I exhaled—"let's say you have good instincts."

"Bob thinks so," she said. Her keys rang as she picked them up. "Damn. Another code. See you in twelve."

67

MAY 23, 04:21

HOPE

I sat tight. At least most of my skin had dried, leaving my underclothes damp and clammy.

My pager went off.

"We need you," a nurse said, her voice low and unfamiliar.

"OR 3?" I squeaked.

"Pronto." She hung up.

I swore. I'd played it safe up until now, but this nurse forced my hand.

I tiptoed to the door, clothes hanger in my left hand. "Is anybody there?" I asked quietly.

No one answered.

Normally, I'd hear call room noises: other pagers ringing, sleepy voices answering calls, toilets flushing, doors slamming, even their mattresses creaking as they turned over.

Right now, an eerie hush greeted my ears, as if all the birds had fallen silent in the forest before a predator.

I straightened the curved hook of the wire hanger so it stuck out straight and I could jab someone's eye with it. Switching my primitive weapon to my right hand, I used my non-dominant one to twist open the door.

The pile of clothes flopped over, a ball of socks rolling toward me. I reached for them.

A woman shot out from behind the door clutching a syringe.

I gasped and dropped the socks. Dropped the wire hanger too, damn it, but I grasped the door handle with both hands and rammed her with the wood, trying to knock her out and slam it shut.

She dropped the syringe with a muffled curse, but seized the other side of the door handle with both hands.

"HELP HELP HELP HELP HELP!" I screamed as she yanked the door towards her, wrenching it from my grasp.

She was stronger than me. Most people are.

I changed tactics and flung the door toward her instead, surprising her into a step back.

I screamed wordlessly and dashed into the hallway, turning right. Away from her.

I took the stairs barefoot, wincing, but I couldn't worry about bacteria and needlesticks right now. Must. Get. Away.

I might be barefoot, but not bare-assed. Thank you, bra and panties, even though the latter gave me a wedgie as I hustled down another floor.

She paused, and I knew she'd scooped up her syringe.

Good news: she lost a few crucial seconds.

Bad news: she'd recovered her means to kill me.

I barrelled down the sixth and last flight, huffing toward the emergency room. No fucking way I'd hit the relatively unfamiliar territory of the surgical suites, where Dr. Vrac might take my undress as an invitation.

I tore straight for the ER with Roxanne and Andrea, the security guards, dozens of waiting patients, and the smell of poo and pus. Home.

I'd dropped my precious phone somewhere en route. No time to cry about it.

As I sprinted past the line of sleepy ER patients in their hallway gurneys, I nearly bowled over a middle-aged man in a guard uniform who held a patient's gown in his hands. I yanked it from his arms and said, "Call 911, Frank!"

Frank gaped at me in my underwear.

I kept running and tossed over my shoulder, "She's coming after us! She's got a syringe!"

"Who?" he asked.

"Call 911. She's already killed, or almost killed, two men!"

The killer's voice rang out behind me, out of breath but still authoritative. "Who are you calling?"

"She said 911," said Frank.

"She's crazy. Look at her, running around in her underwear."

I swore and turned the corner, toward the guard's booth between the main ER doors and patient registration, but I still heard Frank ask, "Why do you have a syringe?"

Fuck.

If she killed him ...

But she could kill me.

And I didn't have my phone.

Shit, shit, shit.

"HELP HELP HELP HELP HELP!" I yelled, turning back to help Frank and face my nemesis.

A wrinkled patient squinted at me from under her nest of blankets. "I'm trying to sleep, girlie."

"She's trying to *kill* us! Call 911!"

The old lady considered it. "What do I say?"

"Tammy, the OR charge nurse, has a syringe. She already stabbed Dr. Burns. She may be killing a guard right now. Please!"

The lady smacked her lips and dredged a brand new phone out from her bra. "So no one will steal it," she explained.

"Yes! Great! Please!"

Too late for the guard. I heard Frank groan behind us.

The other patients goggled at me. "Call for help!" I shouted, miming a phone to my ear for those who didn't speak English, and nearly popping my left breast out. An old man reached for his phone, but I was afraid it was to film me instead of calling 911.

I hurried toward the ER's automatic doors when footsteps burst toward me. I spun around to confront Tammy, but Nikki Burns tossed a bag of clothes in my arms.

"You weren't kidding about the nakedness," Nikki said.

I caught the clothes but punched open the ER door. "She's right behind me."

Nikki's eyes narrowed. "Who did this."

"Tammy. With a syringe."

"That fucking bitch tried to kill *Bobby.*" She set straight down the hallway, toward Tammy instead of away.

"Nikki, call 911!"

Nikki marched onward, the heels of her ankle boots clicking on the tile floor.

"I'm already calling them," the elderly female patient cackled. "I'm on hold."

"On hold? There's no hold for 911."

She stared at her phone and held it up to me to verify.

Who the hell had she called?

Should I run to the ER to activate 911, or back up Nikki and the guard barehanded?

The other patients blinked at me now, puzzled at my gown and commands. Who'd disturbed them, if not for a meal, vitals, or pills?

"Call 911!" I told them. "Please. We've had multiple murders at the hospital tonight."

The "Still working?" woman in casts nodded at her pillow. "You take my phone. I'll give you my code."

"Thank you!"

I entered her phone PIN, called 911 for her on speakerphone, and dashed back into the main hallway for Nikki and Frank, praying it wasn't too late.

Frank lay on the ground, unmoving. My heart plunged.

Nikki faced Tammy, only six feet away from her. Neither of them spoke, but they circled each other like lionesses, silent and murderous.

I checked Tammy for weapons. She'd used one syringe on the

guard and must've stuck Gordon with another, but she carried two more in her front pocket. Jesus. Like an assault rifle with backup ammo. How many people did she plan to kill right now?

"Why did you do it, Tammy?" I called, trying to distract her.

Instead of answering, she withdrew the second-last syringe from her pocket, still circling Nikki.

"Yeah, bitch!" called Nikki. "Why'd you kill my husband?"

"Is he dead?" Tammy's eyes flickered as she uncapped her syringe.

"Wouldn't you like to know."

Although she kept her eyes on Nikki, Tammy crooked her finger, signalling me to come. My mind flashed to the fairy tales where the evil witch beckons you forth.

I shook my head.

"You ruined *everything,"* Tammy spat at me.

And I would have gotten away with it too, if it hadn't been for you meddling kids!

"How did it work?" Nikki wondered aloud. "You and Vrac, huh? I thought he liked the young birds."

Tammy's mouth drew back into a rictus.

"'Course you were young once," Nikki cooed. "Was that when you had your own private Vrac attack?"

I exhaled softly.

"You've been working at UC for a dog's age before you came to St. Joe's. Even though you harass nurses about time off, I know you took 10 months off, years ago. For a baby?"

"None of your fucking business," said Tammy.

"Language." Nikki smiled sweetly at her. "I'd swear too if I'd had Vrac's secret love child. Been raising him all this time with no support from him, huh? While he donates $50K to the hospital foundation here and $75K to UC to cover up his abuse?" Nikki whistled.

Patients chattered on their cell phones, but I didn't hear sirens. We'd have to delay Tammy even longer.

Nikki showed her teeth. "That would bother me, but I guess you like playing the long game, Tamster. How old's your kid now? Fifteen?"

Tammy's hands clawed into fists.

"You're not retirement age yet. Your son's looking at university now, huh? That's when kids get really expensive. Although I can't believe you did everything on your own up until now. Did you have a nanny? That costs. Meanwhile, Vrac's buying a car a week and shtupping any girl within a six foot radius. He's laughing while you're working day and night and never get to see your kid. But you can stand it as long as Vrac's your golden ticket out for you and your son. What's your boy's name again?"

Tammy's mouth shaped sounds I didn't understand.

Nikki had years of practice talking to semi-conscious patients, and she probably knew it already. "Jasha. A nice Russian name in honour of his daddy.'"

Tammy's cheeks turned a dull red. "That's not it."

"I know all about Vladimir, Waldo, Vadim, and Vance Vrac. He likes to change his name, huh? Covers a multitude of sins."

Tammy used her left hand to balance the syringe in the air while she placed her right hand on the plunger. I tensed.

"You're going to throw that at me like a dart?" Nikki cocked her head to the side. "I guess you could. But you need to push the plunger down or the medication doesn't go in. And you want to make sure it goes IM or subQ, right? Can't count on piercing a vein at five paces."

Tammy stepped toward her, trying to trap Nikki between herself and the wall.

Nikki slid sideways, maintaining the distance, cool as you please.

"Stay back." I called to Tammy's back while I glanced around the hallway for a weapon.

The old male patient had crept out of his stretcher so he could film everything. "I got it!" he mouthed at me.

I held a finger to my lips and pointed at his stretcher at the end of the hallway closest to me, where his blankets lay in a bundle.

He nodded, so I carefully lifted the brakes off and rolled his stretcher away from the wall.

Nikki's eyes flashed in comprehension although she kept her gaze trained on Tammy, distracting the OR charge nurse. "Got a hammer, everything looks like a nail, eh Tam-Tam? Inject one, inject 'em all, am I right? But you've got to think about Jasha."

Tammy's nostrils flared. "Don't you say his name."

"You thought you'd make one happy family. Doesn't work when Daddy gets charged with killing Joan Finn—"

"Vlad's innocent!"

Sirens wailed faintly in the distance.

Please, please please be police and not another ambulance backlogging the ER.

Nikki rolled her eyes. "I read both autopsy reports. We paid for a private autopsy after the official one, did you know that? It won't come out until the trial. Who'll look after Jasha when Vrac's locked up and you go down for attempted murder and brib—"

Tammy lowered her head and charged Nikki like a rhino while I rushed at Tammy with the bed.

Too fast and I might seriously hurt Tammy. Too gentle, and I'd lose my advantage. Tammy might even turn the bed against me. She'd already proven her superior strength at the call room.

I gritted my teeth, elbows braced, bed flying while Nikki slipped away from the wall at the last second. "Ha!"

Tammy whirled around at the sound of the wheels. She stumbled, snarled, and threw her hands up against the wall to break her fall, the naked fury in her eyes almost paralyzing me for a crucial second.

Then I hurled the short side of the bed into Tammy's hips. She keeled over it, hinging forward with a howl and catching herself on the mattress. I hadn't hit her hard enough to break her hips, and too low to paralyze her diaphragm as Vrac had mine.

Perfect shot to pin her against the wall.

Nikki rushed to my side, chuckling with delight, as she battered the bed against Tammy's hips one more time.

Tammy's bones crunched a split second before Tammy herself screamed in rage.

"That was for Bobby." Nikki set the brakes with a stomp of her boot.

Tammy lunged to strike her with the syringe, but gasped as her hips stayed fixed in place.

"Booyah, bitch!" Nikki called, dancing out of the way. "You might have snuck up on Bobby, but I've got you pinned like a butterfly, stung like a bee!"

"Assault," Tammy ground out, tears glittering in her eyes.

"MURDERER," Nikki returned, right before the police filled the hall behind us and I rushed to start the code on Frank.

68

MAY 23, 08:57

HOPE

"I'm sorry I missed it," Tucker said after my teaching rounds on diverticular disease. We dropped into the cafeteria before returning to our rotations. I couldn't leave Cheng to cover the wards alone post-call, even though I desperately craved sleep. Tucker had insisted on buying me a coffee so I didn't nod off before someone could cover me.

"Me too," said Tori, stealing a home fry from Griffin.

Griffin pushed a muffin toward Tori and another toward me. "Sorry, bro," he told Tucker. "Didn't know you were coming."

Tucker shrugged and showed him a granola bar he'd hidden in his pocket. "Save it for the pretty women. They did all the work."

I borrowed some of Tori's hand sanitizer before biting into the muffin and pushing five bucks toward Griffin. "Thanks. I really needed this."

Griffin pushed it back. "You earned it, girl."

I laughed, not entirely immune to Griffin's Asian eyes and dark skin, though of course I'd never poach my friend's man.

Tucker took a swig of water from a bottle he'd tucked in his white coat pocket. "Seriously, Hope, you get all the fun."

"Fun?" The official toxicology reports wouldn't come back from

Tammy's syringes for days or weeks, but Frank the guard had required intubation. We suspected Rocuronium or another paralytic, same as Dr. Burns. And same as Gordon. "Like risking paralysis by a madwoman?"

"In your underwear," Tucker agreed.

My turn to blush, even though I'd donned Nikki's loose black top and pants and my backup shoes. "You're never going to let me forget that, are you?"

"Never." His left eye dropped in a wink.

I beamed. At least he talked to me now, plus a little extra.

"If you've finished flirting," said Tori demurely, "Roy messaged me. He'll testify—anonymously, if possible—that Dr. Vrac, his treating physician, prescribed him dangerous quantities of opioids and underpaid him for car repair work that always stayed off the books. I wonder if Mireille wasn't his first hit and run."

I shook my head and chewed my banana muffin, too tired for outrage. "Will Roy get in trouble?"

"He might," said Tori, "but our society understands addiction a bit more, and Roy's so relieved to get away from Dr. Vrac that I think he'll testify even if it puts himself and his garage at risk."

Which made me think of Singh. Escape from Vrac at any cost. What about Singh's parents? Any brothers or sisters? How scared must Roy have been to cover up Vrac's crimes almost for free, and Singh for nothing at all? My muffin started back up, and I hid my face with a napkin as I choked it back down.

Tori laid a hand on my arm. "Maybe you can speak to Raj's family and bring them some comfort."

"Maybe." I wiped my eyes with the napkin. I'd turn my muffin salty at this rate.

Tori changed the subject. "I got one last visit from our motorcyclist last night."

A farewell from the ghost. "The motorcycler spoke to you?" When Tucker smiled, I said, "I mean motorcyclist."

She shook her head. "But that person is more at rest now, too. I understand that his stepfather tried to save money by doing the repairs himself, using a chain from another kind of motorcycle and not installing it right. The chain snapped."

The stepfather killed Vrac's brother? Even by accident? My mouth dropped open.

Tori cast me a warning look and I sipped my coffee, trying to understand Vrac.

Tucker's brow wrinkled. "I hate that guy with the fire of a thousand burning suns. Still, Vrac's carried that his whole life."

"No excuses," Griffin agreed, "but that guy needs *a lot* of therapy."

"So much," I agreed. Vlad Vrac and his murder cars, running over witnesses in the streets and crushing their spirits in the OR.

I checked my pager. No pages, so Cheng had shouldered twice the calls while I learned about diverticulitis. I stood up. "Is Mireille okay?"

"She texted me this morning. Sounded all right," said Tucker.

"She's not supposed to text!" I objected.

Tucker lifted his shoulders. "She said she'd gotten hit around 6 a.m., making it over 24 hours since her concussion."

Yeah, Mireille had turned the corner. I mentally saluted her. She'd testify against Vrac.

"Dr. Burns is stable in the unit too," Tucker said.

I nearly smiled. "He doesn't dare die with Nikki on the case."

"She's a phenom," Tucker said.

Tori turned to me. "Did you really trap the OR charge nurse against the wall with a patient bed?"

"Nikki helped," I said. "Not glamorous, but it kept her at arms' length from both of us."

Tucker struggled not to laugh around his granola bar.

"Not funny!" I told him.

"Not funny at all," he said, turning down the corners of his mouth.

I cackled first. "On my first day in general surgery, the attending grabbed my ass and the OR charge nurse technically killed the anesthetist. Then the attending ran over his former med student, killed the scrub nurse, and bullied his chief resident into committing suicide, after they all witnessed him mismanaging a case. The OR charge nurse tried to kill a resident, a guard, and me while I ran outside the ER in my underwear. I think that's a new low, even for me."

"Oh, I don't know." Tucker grinned widely now. "You earned a lot of new fans. The patients waiting for admission were still talking about it when I walked by. Best thing that ever happened to them."

I covered my face. At least I could give a statement to the police fully-dressed.

"I don't understand why Tammy would attack so many people," said Tori.

"Me neither." I sighed. "She does have a kid with Vrac. They got it on back in the day. Tammy wanted Jasha, their kid, to follow in Daddy's footsteps and become a surgeon. She messaged Vrac anonymously to pay up. Child support, university, med school. The whole shebang."

"Anonymously?" Tucker frowned.

"Yeah, I guess watching him chase young scrub nurses made her hide her ID. But Tammy finally came forward and got a paternity test out of him." I hesitated. "Nikki's PI noted a huge deposit to Tammy's bank account yesterday at lunchtime."

"Whoa," said Tucker.

Griffin shook his head. "Bank accounts are private. You saying what I think you're saying?"

I nodded. "Vrac bribed her to help kill all the witnesses."

Griffin raised his eyebrows. "If they can prove that deposit came from Vrac, we've got 'em."

I shredded my muffin liner. "Tammy probably thought she'd get back together with him someday, but she found Vrac in freefall with a lawsuit about to end his surgical career. She made the deal with him for extra cash, plus killing the witnesses meant he'd keep on operating. Her goose would keep laying golden eggs."

Griffin shook his head. "She should've made up a secret bank account, though."

"Maybe her strength was organizing OR schedules, not subterfuge," I said.

Tori added softly, "I heard a theory that criminals do stupid things because they secretly want to get caught. They feel guilty."

"I can see that," said Tucker. "You know, Gordon messaged Vrac anonymously too."

"What?" I snapped my neck toward him.

"Yeah, I feel bad for Gordon." Tucker shook his head. "We go back a few years. He's a good guy. Gordon denied actually threatening him, but he pressured Vrac to do the right thing by Joan Finn and her family. Take responsibility for her death instead of blaming Gordon and Dr. Burns. Then Gordon figured out that Vrac added Gogolax and other laxatives to Dr. Burns's lunch."

Tori's eyes bugged out.

I brightened instead. "I'm sure that's against the law. We can nail him on that too!"

Tucker shook his head. "Gordon can't prove it. After the fact, Vrac got Singh to tamper with Burns's food."

"Singh?" I whispered, my heart dropping like an engine block.

Tucker winced. "Yeah. It's in Singh's last note. He swears he didn't alter any food before the surgery, but Vrac forced him to do it at least once later. That was after Gordon had set up a camera and recorded Singh doing it. Gordon tried to talk to Singh about it, because Singh was always a decent guy, but the video's one more thing that drove Singh over the edge."

My fists knotted. I paced around the table, trying not to punch the wall or scream. "That bastard set Singh up to take the fall and then blackmailed him. No wonder Vrac thought he could puncture the spleen on camera and get away with it. He had Singh by the entrails!"

Tori stood up too. "Vrac can't hurt him anymore."

I dug my nails into my own palms, concentrating on the pain so I wouldn't lose it in front of the entire cafeteria. I squeezed my eyes shut. "Vrac's still alive. It's not fair. It's not fair. It's *not fair."*

"No," Tucker agreed, "but Singh also included detailed notes on every patient Vrac mismanaged, complete with ID numbers and dates. I guarantee you more lawsuits. He'll lose his privileges and his license to practice."

I plunked back into my chair, its legs screeching on the brown tile floor. "He'll hire the most expensive lawyer to protect him."

"You'll all testify against him," said Tori. "Cheng. Nikki. Dr. Burns. Mireille. You."

"We will," I vowed.

"Gordon too," said Tucker. "Tammy tried to kill him, but he made it. I'll introduce the two of you. You'll like him."

I smiled. "I kinda like him already. And you."

Tucker met my eyes with his deep brown ones.

"All of you," I added quickly, blowing everyone a kiss to cover the awkward moment.

Before I rose from the table, I locked eyes with Tori. Her pupils dilated, and I immediately smelled blood.

"What is it?" Tucker's voice echoed off my skull, but the jolt of pain across the base of my neck muted me.

"Hope?"

Agony shot down both my arms, followed by a shock wave of numbness. I bit back a howl.

"Is she having a seizure?"

"My hands," I muttered. "My fucking *hands.*"

"Hope?" Tucker reached for me, but I twitched away as best I could with both my hands trapped under the dashboard. Couldn't move my legs either. Fuck. Fuck fuck fuck fuck FUCK.

"Hope. You're okay," said Tori. "I feel it too."

"Mikhail? That you?" I called. "You made me crash my fuckin' Audi."

"Vrac crashed his car," Tori murmured to the men, and repeated it louder, to me, while squeezing my hand. "It's not *you,* Hope. You're here with me and Tucker and Griffin. You're safe."

"Hope you're happy, bro. See you in hell," I hissed back.

Cold water splashed my face, my glasses, and even up my nose and in my mouth, stunning me out of the Audi's shattered glass and metal cage, back into the cafeteria.

The entire caf silently stared at me. One customer peered from the other end of the room while her phone squawked in the air.

"Sorry." Tori handed Tucker back his water bottle with a guilty expression.

I glanced down at my dripping torso, trying to piece together what happened.

"What the ... " Tucker whispered.

"Vrac got a visit from his brother and crashed his Audi," Tori repeated, and I finally understood. Somehow, I'd been transported inside that mofo's body at that crucial second, suspending me between the car wreckage and the hospital cafeteria, in both worlds and in neither at the same time.

Welded to the world's most evil surgeon.

"Hold up," said Tucker, eyes narrowed as he tried to process this. "You ... and Vrac? And Tori? Sort of brain twins now?"

Griffin handed me napkins.

"Brain triplets, if anything." I used the napkins to wipe my eyes and face, but an even more terrible thought almost made me drop my glasses. "What if you hadn't broken me out?" I asked Tori.

Tori licked her lips. "But I did."

"Would I have stayed trapped with Vrac forever? What if he *died?* Would I go with him?" I clung to my glasses and inhaled the soggy napkin. More CO_2 to calm down. Or maybe asphyxiation.

See you in hell.

I dropped the napkin on the table. "Or to prison. Even if he got free and kept torturing residents, I don't want that man inside my head. Ever."

"I know," said Tori. "Me neither. Don't worry, Hope. We'll figure it out."

I covered my face while she and Tucker hugged me, trying to comfort me with their bodies.

I clung to both of them for a minute, breathing in Tori's shampoo and Tucker's musk. My friends. My former lover and fiancé. My family away from home.

Griffin offered me more napkins over their heads, making me smile.

Then I strode back to the surgery ward, calling Cheng to see what I'd missed.

ACKNOWLEDGMENTS

I write to you from the days of rage of 2022. "Entitled" and "burnout" come up over and over again online. This inspired my new Hope series, each book outlining one of the seven deadly sins, beginning with wrath.

I haven't hit the OR in years and take full responsibility for any errors. Copious thanks to RN Carolyn Baker-Stirling, who answered my questions immediately, and four physicians who offered feedback as soon as I asked: anesthesiologists Dr. Crystal Chettle and Dr. Shona Nair and general surgeons Dr. Eileen Sacks and Dr. Sailaja Nallapaneni. Dr. Nicole Shadbolt speed read through it all the way from Bangladesh!

Even more physicians stepped up in the home stretch, including Drs. Ming-Ka Chan, Marie-Luce Chen, Sylvie Caissie, Kate Ryans, Miriam Berchuk, Kirsten Duckitt, Kim Alexander, Rebecca Lys, Karen Loo, M. Hanley, TL Stothart, Siobhán Muldowney, and more, from anesthesia to family medicine, OR assist, developmental pediatrics, gynecology, ER, and the coroner's unit.

Extra special kudos to Marie-Luce and Eileen who checked it twice, E again for the splenic puncture, and Crystal and Kate for some higher level anesthesia fine-tuning. #absolutelyfabulous

I joined a new group, Thriller-tique, run by the International Thriller Writers. Thank you, Susan, Laura, Lynette, David, Tony, Rick, Steve, and of course ITW. Terrific organization.

I'm perennially grateful to Kathleen Costa for her incisive feedback and to Margaret MacDonald and Dawn Kiddell for copyediting. Thanks to author Ezekiel James Boston for digging me out of plot holes.

Surgeons pointed out that "the evil surgeon" is a harmful stereotype they must combat every day. Please understand that Dr. Vrac is a fictional character who experienced trauma, compounds it, and throws it on the next generation.

That said, I made up some components, but not all of them. A med school classmate described the sterile punch. Several other colleagues knew the "sterile slap." Surgery is brutal.

Every year, suicide kills physicians. Female physicians are over twice as likely to kill themselves as non-physicians. Men are 40 percent more at risk. Every day, we lose more than one physician a day to suicide in the US alone.

In Canada, find help here: https://www.cma.ca/supportline. In the US, call the National Suicide Prevention Lifeline: (800) 273-8255. Let me know of any global resources.

This novel may help you understand why we're at high risk. Not only do we lack the time to see a family doctor to catch problems early, we risk losing our right to practice medicine if our licensing body labels us unfit. We may not have friends or family to support us between work schedules and moving for training. The general public seems not to care, claiming, "You signed up for this." Meanwhile, our anatomy and physiology classes taught us more efficient ways to kill ourselves.

So I beg physicians, nurses, and everyone in these tumultuous times to seek help. You deserve to live. Heal thyself.

Anger is a double-edged sword. Too little and you risk drowning in passivity. Too much and you immolate yourself and everyone in your path. I strive for a judicious amount of anger, like pepper in a stew. Enough to wake up, but not so much that I can't taste anything else.

If you enjoyed *The Shapes of Wrath*, please leave a review, subscribe to my newsletter, and buckle up for the next deadly sin with Hope in 2023.

Wishing you just enough wrath,

Melissa

ABOUT THE AUTHOR

Melissa Yi is an emergency doctor with an award-winning writing career.

If you enjoyed The Shapes of Wrath—and who can resist a good ragefest—please post a review!

Join the KamikaSze newsletter at www.myi.ninja *for weirdness and laughter*

amazon.com/author/myi
facebook.com/MelissaYiYuanInnes
twitter.com/dr_sassy
bookbub.com/authors/melissa-yi
instagram.com/melissa.yuaninnes
pinterest.com/melissayi_

ALSO BY MELISSA YI

Hope Sze Medical Crime

Hope Sze novels Amazon series link: https://amzn.to/2GmIKUM

Flamingo Flamenco (Hope Sze short story)

No Air (Hope Sze radio drama)

Code Blues (Hope Sze 1)

Notorious D.O.C. (Hope Sze 2)

Family Medicine (essay & Hope Sze novella combining the short stories *Cain and Abel, Trouble and Strife, and Butcher's Hook*, which are also available separately)

Terminally Ill (Hope Sze 3)

Student Body (Hope Sze novella post-Terminally Ill; includes radio drama *No Air*)

Blood Diamonds (Hope Sze short story)

The Sin Eaters (Hope Sze short story)

Stockholm Syndrome (Hope Sze 4)

Human Remains (Hope Sze 5)

Blue Christmas (Hope Sze short story)

Death Flight (Hope Sze 6)

Graveyard Shift (Hope Sze 7)

Scorpion Scheme (Hope Sze 8)

White Lightning (Hope Sze 9)

Hope's Seven Deadly Sins Thrillers

The Shapes of Wrath (Hope Sins 1)

More mystery & romance novels by Melissa Yi

The Italian School for Assassins *(Octavia & Dario Killer School Mystery 1)*

The Goa Yoga School of Slayers *(Octavia & Dario Killer School Mystery 2)*

Wolf Ice

High School Hit List

The List

Dancing Through the Chaos

Scintillating Speculative Fiction series

Chinese Cinderella, Fairy Godfathers & Beastly Beauty

Dog vs. Aliens, Grandma Othello & Shaolin Monks in Space

Tiger Girls & Vulture Gods

Unfeeling Doctor Series (Melissa Yuan-Innes)

The Most Unfeeling Doctor in the World and Other True Tales From the Emergency Room (Unfeeling Doctor #1)

The Unfeeling Doctor, Unplugged: More True Tales From Med School and Beyond (Unfeeling Doctor #2)

The Unfeeling Wannabe Surgeon: A Doctor's Medical School Memoir (Unfeeling Doctor #3)

The Unfeeling Thousandaire: How I Made $10,000 Indie Publishing and You Can, Too! (Unfeeling Doctor #4)

Buddhish: Exploring Buddhism in a Time of Grief: One Doctor's Story (Unfeeling Doctor #5)

The Unfeeling Doctor Betwixt Birthing Babies: Poems About Love, Loss, and More Love (Unfeeling Doctor #6)

The Knowledgeable Lion: Poems and Prose by the Unfeeling Doctor in Africa (Unfeeling Doctor #7)

Fifty Shades of Grey's Anatomy: The Unfeeling Doctor's Fresh Confessions from the Emergency Room (Unfeeling Doctor #8)

Broken Bones: New True Noir Essays From the Emergency Room by the Most Unfeeling Doctor in the World (Unfeeling Doctor #9)

The Emergency Doctor's Guide Series (Melissa Yuan-Innes)

The Emergency Doctor's Guide to a Pain-Free Back: Fast Tips and Exercises for Healing and Relief

The Emergency Doctor's Guide to Healing Dry Eyes

Let us go forth with fear and courage and rage to save the world.

— Grace Paley